"Fancy a turn around the floor with me?"

"Oh!" Damaris seemed startled. "I don't—"

"I'm a fair dancer. I promise not to step on your wee feet."

"My feet aren't wee and I'm more likely to step on yours. I haven't danced in…I can't remember the last time. And I wasn't very good at it then, either. You might want to ask someone else."

Rory smiled.

"What?"

"Didn't you see me vault clear over that beast today?"

"Well, yes, but—"

"You can't do worse than that. I expect you'll do much better." He stood and held out his hand. "Gather your courage and dance with me, lass."

A COWBOY'S WORTH

THE MCGAVIN BROTHERS

Vicki Lewis Thompson

Ocean Dance Press

Want more cowboys? Check out these other titles by Vicki Lewis Thompson

The McGavin Brothers
A Cowboy's Strength
A Cowboy's Honor
A Cowboy's Return
A Cowboy's Heart
A Cowboy's Courage
A Cowboy's Christmas
A Cowboy's Kiss
A Cowboy's Luck
A Cowboy's Charm
A Cowboy's Challenge
A Cowboy's Baby
A Cowboy's Holiday
A Cowboy's Choice
A Cowboy's Worth

Thunder Mountain Brotherhood
Midnight Thunder
Thunderstruck
Rolling Like Thunder
A Cowboy Under the Mistletoe
Cowboy All Night
Cowboy After Dark
Cowboy Untamed
Cowboy Unwrapped
In the Cowboy's Arms
Say Yes to the Cowboy
Do You Take This Cowboy?

Sons of Chance
Wanted!

Ambushed!
Claimed!
Should've Been a Cowboy
Cowboy Up
Cowboys Like Us
Long Road Home
Lead Me Home
Feels Like Home
I Cross My Heart
Wild at Heart
The Heart Won't Lie
Cowboys and Angels
Riding High
Riding Hard
Riding Home
A Last Chance Christmas

1

Look afore you leap, lad. But where was the fun in that? Rory McGavin had been ignoring his da's advice for years. No point in heeding it now.

That said, his palms were slippery with sweat as he drove down a Montana highway on the wrong bloody side of the road. At the airport in Bozeman, jetlagged and disoriented, he'd climbed into his rental without thinking. Whoops. No steering wheel.

The rental agent had ducked his head as Rory had given him a sheepish grin before sliding out and walking around to the steering wheel side. He'd shoe-horned himself into the driver's seat, said a prayer and pulled into traffic. Navigating had been a nail-biter, despite the bonnie voice on his trusty phone providing directions.

The highway was easier, although delivery trucks big as warehouses swept past, buffeting his wee vehicle. Cowboys drove muscular pickups. He'd learned that from the movies, and sure enough, this highway was full of them. He'd do better against the massive commercial trucks if he had a pickup.

But that hadn't been an option at the rental place. He had a Stetson, though. It rested on the passenger seat because he didn't have enough headroom to wear it in the car.

On impulse, he'd located a Western wear shop on his phone and driven there after he got his rental. He looked good in the hat, if he did say so. His American relations might mistake him for a cowpoke passing through.

Until he opened his mouth, anyway. His brogue would give him away. He couldn't wait to see their faces when he announced who he was. His da and his grandparents had left Montana more than thirty years ago. His Uncle Ian, God rest his soul, had stayed behind, crazy in love with a girl named Kendra. And the rest, as they said, was family history.

The outskirts of Eagles Nest appeared, soothing his jangled nerves. This was more like it. A single street through the village, cheerful shops along either side, folks strolling the sidewalk, many of them wearing hats like his. He looked forward to making new friends in this place.

He passed a bakery named Pie in the Sky and eased up on the gas as his stomach rumbled. No time for pastries, though. Once he located the ranch and connected with his relations, he'd explore the area.

Pills and Pop was likely a pharmacy, should he need one. He slowed again as he neared the Guzzling Grizzly. With that name it had to be a pub. Or maybe folks called it a saloon out here. A pint would sure taste good right now, but beer and jetlag was a bad combination.

The view expanded on the far side of the village—plenty of open country flanked by the tallest mountains he'd ever seen. Snow gleamed on peaks bathed in spring sunshine. He'd been too excited to sleep much on the plane. Adrenaline would have to carry him through until bedtime, because it was midday here.

The voice on his phone warned him of the turnoff to Wild Creek Ranch but he would have noticed it regardless. The wooden sign was decorated with bows, balloons and flower garlands. Had someone tipped them off that he was coming?

Eager though he was to find out, he took the dirt road slower than a pie-eyed bloke stumbling home at dawn. His wee car wasn't built for the ruts.

Eventually he arrived at the ranch. It looked like a movie set—rustic barn, wooden corrals and a low-slung log house complete with rocking chairs lined up on a generous front porch.

The parking area was a sea of pickups. His kinfolks must have gone against his wishes and alerted the McGavins that he was arriving. So much for his big surprise. Then again, walking into a house as the long-anticipated Scottish guest would be all right, too.

He squeezed his wee car into a parking spot, grabbed his new hat and started up to the house. The porch was decorated with more balloons, ribbons and garlands. To his left, a picnic area had flowers on every table. These folks had pulled out all the stops for a visiting relation.

Should he have brought gifts? Maybe, but he'd been in a bit of a rush to leave. Angry people on his trail and all that. But gifts would have been a nice touch seeing as how they'd gone to a great deal of trouble to welcome him.

Taking a breath, he climbed the porch steps and used the metal door knocker in the shape of a coiled lariat.

A woman opened the massive door and stared at him with eyes bluer than the deepest loch in Scotland. "Are you from the florist?"

He'd heard about those blue eyes that had captured his Uncle Ian's heart. Must be Kendra. Evidently the hat had fooled her into thinking he was a delivery boy. "Nay, I'm—"

"Are they here?" A woman about his age appeared behind Kendra. Her dark hair tumbled to her shoulders in glossy waves and she wore a green dressing gown with mathematical equations on it. She squinted at him. "Where are the bouquets?"

"He's not from the florist."

"Then who the heck is he?"

"I have no idea."

"I'm Rory McGavin." He grinned and took off his hat.

The equation lass stepped closer and peered at him. "You're from *Scotland*?"

"Aye." Why wouldn't she know? "Inverness. I'm—"

"You're my nephew?" Kendra's eyes widened. "Hamish and Greer's son?"

"Yes, and I—"

"Good grief! Come here." She pulled him through the door and into a hug. "Why didn't you let us know you were coming?"

"Thought it would be fun to surprise you." Clearly the decorations *weren't* for him.

"You most certainly did surprise me!" She closed the door. "Are you here for the wedding? I didn't bother your folks with an invitation because I didn't think they'd be able to—"

"What weddin'?"

"Ryker's!"

"Ryker! Good for him." That explained the ribbons and balloons. His Uncle Ian and Kendra had been blessed with several sons, at least four or five. His information on his cousins was spotty and he hadn't had time to question his parents. He wouldn't be able to name those boys if his life depended on it.

"It is good. He's marrying his high school sweetheart at long last. April finally agreed to a wedding." Kendra stepped back and looked him up and down. "Are you saying you just took a notion to come over and hopped on a plane?"

"Somethin like that."

"And you arrived today, of all days."

"Didn't mean to cause extra trouble."

"Not at all! The boys will be excited to meet you. They—"

The dark-haired woman next to her cleared her throat.

"Goodness, where are my manners?" Kendra turned to her. "This is Damaris Gataki, one of April's bridesmaids."

"Pleased to make your acquaintance." Rory held out his hand. "Never met a lass with equations on her dressin' gown."

"Oh." She glanced down as if she'd forgotten she was wearing it. "Gift from a friend." She smiled and gave him a firm handshake. "I love your brogue."

"Thank you." Damaris Gataki had a mouth made for kissin'. Not that he'd be kissin' anyone on this trip unless it was a chaste peck on the cheek.

"You sound just like Jamie," she said. "Look a little like him, too."

"Jamie?"

"*Jamie Fraser*."

"I don't—"

She made an impatient noise. "From *Outlander*."

"Oh." He'd never seen the show but he'd heard about the Scottish bloke who starred in it, mostly from ladies speaking the way Damaris had, like this Jamie was some kind of god.

"No one's ever told you that?"

"Nay. They mention Prince Harry sometimes. Guess it's the ginger hair."

"And the blue eyes. If your hair was a bit longer—"

"'Scuse me, kids, but I think I heard somebody pull up." Kendra opened the door and peeked out. "It's a van. That's promising."

Damaris blinked. "Right. The flowers."

"The guy has a clipboard. I'll bet this is it." Kendra opened the door wider and raised her voice. "Are you from the florist?"

"Yes, ma'am! Sorry about the delay." He slid back the van's side door.

"At least you're here now." Kendra turned to Damaris. "Better go tell April. I'm sure she was freaking out."

"She was, which is why I came to check. See you later, Rory." She started toward the hallway. Then she spun back to face him. "How long are you staying?"

"I'm not sure. It depends on—"

"For a while, then?"

"I hope to."

"Good." She pivoted and hurried down the hall. "April! Flowers are here!"

Kendra looked at him. "She's a big *Outlander* fan."

"Figured that."

"And super smart. She was valedictorian of April and Ryker's class." She tilted her head toward the open door. "If you'll come with me and help carry, it'll go faster."

"Glad to make myself useful." He clapped his hat on and followed her.

She started down the steps. "I'm happy to hear you can stay a while. How are your folks?"

"They're well. Said to give you their best."

"It's a shame we've lost touch over the years. You're about the same age as my boys. I'm sure you'll get along great."

"I expect we will."

"They're all up at Cody's A-frame getting ready. I'd send you up there, but having you appear out of the blue might disrupt the flow and Ryker wants everything to go like clockwork. I could say that he's schedule-oriented because of his Air Force training, but he's always been a man with a plan."

"I'm the exact opposite."

She laughed. "I'm getting that."

* * *

A Jamie Fraser look-alike. What were the chances? And he was sticking around for a while. Damaris was a-okay with that.

The invitation to be a bridesmaid in April's wedding had arrived at a particularly frustrating period in her research. Fortuitous timing. After spending a dozen years in California with only brief visits back to Eagles Nest, she yearned for a dose of its nurturing atmosphere. Her parents didn't live here anymore, but she still thought of it as home.

April had planned the wedding around Caltech's spring break to accommodate her, and Kendra had urged her to stay on after the wedding for some R and R. She'd accepted.

She wasn't great at relaxing, especially when work was tying her in knots. She'd vowed to loosen up by mucking out stalls and taking long horseback rides on familiar trails.

Now it looked as if Wild Creek Ranch would have another house guest, a Scottish ginger with a fetching brogue. Her stay had just become exponentially more interesting.

Nearly everyone in the bridal party was dressed when she arrived to announce that the flowers had arrived. They cheered at the news.

"Wow, you all look gorgeous!" Damaris surveyed the large group of attendants, the consequence of marrying into a big family. "The vintage riding outfits are pure genius."

April smiled. "I can't wait to see you in yours. The green should exactly match your eyes."

"Which reminds me. I need to put my contacts in." She wished she'd had them when she'd met Rory so she could have seen his magnificent self with more clarity.

"Bouquets incoming!" Kendra brought in florist boxes, set them down and went back for the rest.

April's sister Leigh was the matron of honor. Ryker had chosen his Air Force buddy and business partner in Badger Air, Badger Calhoun, as his best man. Damaris was paired with groomsman and Air Force vet, Aaron Donahue, who'd recently moved to Eagles Nest to work for Badger Air. Ryker's brothers made up the rest of the groomsmen contingent and their significant others were all bridesmaids.

In the hubbub that followed as everyone claimed their bouquet, Damaris found a moment to speak to Kendra. "So where's Rory?"

Kendra looked amused. "Liked him, did you?"

"How could I not? He's a Scots ginger."

"I settled him into a bedroom so he'd have a chance to freshen up before the wedding."

Damaris nodded. "Good move." Only one bedroom was available for Rory—the one next to hers. They'd be sharing the hall bathroom, too.

Cozy. "Does he know that most of the guests are riding out to the meadow?"

"I didn't think to tell him, but we should find out whether he rides. If he does, Quinn or Jim will need to saddle another horse. Or he can just take the buckboard."

"I'll bet he'll want to ride." A Jamie Fraser look-alike wouldn't be caught dead taking a buckboard when he could sit astride a high-spirited horse.

"He did arrive wearing a suitable hat. Listen, the Whine and Cheese Club will be here any minute and I still need to change clothes. Would you ask Rory if he wants a horse, and if he does, will you contact Quinn?" She pulled out her phone. "I'm texting you Quinn's number."

Damaris checked her phone. "Got it. I'll handle this. I can make sure Rory is introduced to everyone in the bridal party, too."

"That would be great. Thanks."

"Trust me, it's *not* a hardship."

"Exactly why I asked you." Kendra gave her a quick wink and left the room.

<u>**2**</u>

Rory hadn't packed for a wedding. He'd brought his kilt, only because he never traveled without it and his plaid, but dressing in all his Highland glory would draw too much attention. Jeans and his work boots would have to do, along with his favorite blue plaid flannel shirt. He'd brought a wool sweater, but the day was fine, especially by Scottish standards. He wouldn't need the sweater.

Judging from the increasing noise level in the house as he changed clothes, more folks had arrived. When he emerged, hat in hand, the place was humming. Bonnie lasses had gathered in the living room and laughter spilled from the kitchen.

Kendra was nowhere to be seen, so he headed for the only person he recognized, Damaris the valedictorian. Exchanging the housecoat for a lacy green dress gave him a better idea of her curves, not that he should be letting himself notice curves on this trip, either. She wore a fancy brimmed hat that matched her dress.

She smiled when he approached. "Hey, Rory! Kendra asked me to find out if you want to take the buckboard out to the meadow for the ceremony or ride a horse."

"A horse?"

"See, I knew you'd choose that! I need to text Quinn." She took her phone out of a hidden pocket in her skirt.

"Right. A horse." He knew about buckboards from the movies, too. They were used for hauling things. And people who couldn't ride. That wasn't him. He'd seen it done enough times. Looked easy enough.

But his mount would be chosen by a unknown bloke named Quinn. Must be a stable hand. Should he ask for a gentle beast? Nope. That would brand him as a beginner.

"Done." She tucked her phone away. "We all know who *you* are, so let me make some introductions so you can get acquainted with everyone."

"I'd surely appreciate that."

She turned to the slender brunette in an ivory dress and hat. "We should start with the bride. April and I have been friends since kindergarten."

"Pleased to meet you, April." Rory shook her hand. "Wishin' you great happiness on your weddin' day."

"Thank you." She took his hand in both of hers. "I'm so glad you're here. Ryker will be, too."

"Does he know, yet?"

"I'm not sure. We agreed not to call or text each other today." April glanced at Damaris. "Has anybody told him about Rory?"

"I doubt anyone has," Damaris said. "Everybody's super focused on keeping the schedule."

April laughed. "That's a good thing since we have three military men involved. I've been told it'll start precisely at fourteen-hundred hours or those flyboys will know the reason why."

"Sounds just like those guys, sis. Gotta love 'em." A dark-haired woman in yellow stepped forward. "Welcome to Montana, Rory. I'm April's sister, Leigh."

"Pleased to meet you, Leigh." He shook her hand, as well.

"And this is Mandy," Damaris said. "She's married to your cousin Zane."

"You can remember me because I'm the preggers bridesmaid." Mandy patted her stomach.

"Congratulations! When's your wee bairn due?"

"Fourth of July, not that I'm counting the days or anything. He or she will be your first cousin once removed. But you already have one of those, so this will be the second in line."

Rory struggled to follow that confusing speech. "And who be the other one?"

"My daughter, Noel." A woman with a long blond braid held out her hand. "Glad to meet you, Rory. I'm Faith, Cody's wife."

"Happy to make your acquaintance, Faith. Is your bairn around?"

"She's only four months old, so Gage and Emma are watching her until after the ceremony." She patted his arm. "I know you have no clue who Gage and Emma are, but Noel's in good hands."

"I'll take your word for it." He scrubbed a hand over his face. "Hearin' about all my new relations is a bit overwhelmin'." He hadn't considered that his cousins were of an age to produce more McGavins. He and Aleck were the last of their branch and neither one of them were ready for children.

"This lady in blue is Nicole," Damaris said. "Nicole is engaged to your cousin Bryce, and over here is Olivia, who's engaged to your cousin Trevor."

He gave up trying to keep it all straight. April he'd remember, and Leigh, her sister. Beyond that, he'd lost track. April was marrying Ryker. That much was clear.

The rest of the players were a jumble— Mandy, Faith, Nicole, Olivia...each in a dress and hat of a different color. So many lovely lasses. Zane, Cody, Bryce and Trevor matched up with them somehow. Noel, a first cousin once removed, was four months old already and another one in that category was on the way. It was enough to turn anyone's brain to mush, let alone a poor bloke who'd been traveling for nearly twenty-four hours.

He'd get everything sorted before the day was over, but for now he'd chat with the ladies and be careful not to use their names. He'd mix them up, for sure. Eventually he turned to Damaris, his anchor in this swirling current. "Where's Kendra?"

"In the kitchen with the Whine and Cheese Club."

"Excuse me?" Yes, his head might explode.

"Her four best friends. That's what they call themselves and they're here to help organize the food for the reception."

"My mom's in there, too," April said. "They made her an honorary member for the weekend. My dad and Leigh's husband are up at Cody's A-frame with the other guys."

"And thank God they took Pax." Leigh turned to Rory. "She's our rambunctious almost two-year-old and she dotes on her Uncle Ryker. He located a pony so she can be the flower girl. Under the supervision of her daddy, of course."

"Sounds like it'll be a fun ceremony." With a passel of folks to feed afterward. He glanced around. "Is this where they'll be holdin' the reception?"

"No, it'll be outside, too." Damaris said. "We're so lucky the weather is nice. Unseasonably warm, in fact." Her phone chimed. "That's Quinn about your horse." She consulted the screen. "He wants to know how much riding experience you've had."

"Experience? Well, I suppose—"

"Okay, everyone!" Kendra came out of the kitchen trailed by a lively, pink-cheeked group.

If Rory had to make a guess, he'd say those ladies had been tippling a bit.

Kendra held up her phone. "Badger just texted me that the groom and his entourage are out at the meadow and the guests have nearly all arrived. Time for us to head down to the barn and mount up."

Damaris glanced at Rory. "I'll just text him that you're fine with whatever."

"Good."

She grinned. "I love how you say that. *Gude.* Come on. I'll walk you down there and introduce you to Quinn. He's amazing."

"Has a talent for horses, does he?" He followed her out the door and they joined the parade of ladies trooping to the barn.

"Quinn's a man of many talents," Damaris said. "He's a successful artist, maintains and rides a classic Harley, dances like a pro and has a great sense of humor. No wonder Kendra fell for him."

Kendra was in the lead and far enough away that she wouldn't be able to hear this conversation. Despite the distance, he lowered his voice. "She's in love with her stable hand?"

"Oh, he's not the stable hand. He has his own place across the road, his own barn and his own horses. He's also the only man Kendra's looked at since her husband died." She glanced at him. "I guess that would have been your uncle."

"Aye. Uncle Ian. I never knew him, but my da says he was a fine fellow. Gran and Grandpa say so, too."

"Big shoes to fill, I gather. After he was gone, Kendra spent all her time running this ranch and raising her boys."

"I heard that. My relations speak of her as if she's a superwoman."

"She certainly is. And for years she showed no interest in dating. Then along came Quinn Sawyer and swept her off her feet."

"Why's he livin' across the road, then?"

"They're both strong personalities. They each like their own space."

"Interestin'."

"That's Quinn over there helping April mount up on the palomino. I don't recognize that horse, but he's a beauty. Split skirts can be tricky. But she wanted a vintage theme for the bridal party."

"I like 'em. Practical." Rory smiled as Quinn gave Kendra a quick kiss before boosting her onto a horse splashed with gold and white patches. "Did Quinn put all those ribbons in the manes and tails?"

"That was probably his daughter Roxanne. She's artistic like her dad. Her husband Michael co-owns the Guzzling Grizzly with Bryce McGavin. Did you see it on your way through town?"

"I did. But I'm havin' trouble keepin' these names and faces straight, let alone what each one does for a livin'."

"It's a lot to remember, especially if you're jetlagged," Damaris said.

"That I am, lass. That I am." This hearty clan had him at a disadvantage. Quinn Sawyer was clearly well-rested, though. He cut a fine figure as he helped a woman with long silver hair onto her horse.

"That's April's mother," Damaris said.

"Nice-lookin' lady. It's a handsome bunch." As the rest of the bridal party mounted up, a wagon appeared pulled by two horses and driven by a lanky cowboy who looked to be about Quinn's age. "Must be the buckboard."

"Yep. Caitlin requested it for her photography gear, which solved another problem.

Judy and Christine from the Whine and Cheese Club don't ride and neither do their husbands. They all decided to take the buckboard, too."

"Ah." The folks she'd mentioned climbed in. Then the driver said something to Quinn, slapped the reins against the horses' rumps and started off.

"That's Jim driving the buckboard. He's Faith's dad."

"Mm."

Damaris looked up at him. "Are you okay? You look a little dazed."

He sighed. "Likely because I am a wee bit dazed. Feel like I've jumped into the deep end of the gene pool."

"Take a long, slow breath. Oxygenate."

He did as she suggested, filling his lungs with cool, fresh air and gradually letting it out.

"Better?"

"I am. Thanks."

"I just thought of something that might help you."

"What's that?"

"I haven't lived here since high school, so when April invited me to be in the wedding, I asked for a list of everyone I'd be meeting and snapshots if she had them. Then I created an updatable spreadsheet. I've added details as I learn them. It's all on my phone. If you want, I could help you navigate through the names and faces today."

A spreadsheet? Bloody brilliant. Armed with that, he might survive the day without his head exploding. "That would be a blessin'. My brain feels as dense as a bowl of cold porridge."

"Stick with me and you'll be fine."

"That's generous, lass, but I don't want to be a bother. If you sent that spreadsheet to my phone you wouldn't have to—"

"It's no bother." Her green gaze warmed. "I'd be happy to serve as your official guide."

Such bonnie eyes. And tempting mouth…

"Quinn's calling us."

"Oh." He glanced toward the barn.

"Everyone's mounted except you, me and him." She raised her voice. "We're on our way, Quinn!"

Rory walked with her toward three saddled horses tied to the hitching post in front of the barn.

Damaris swept a hand in his direction. "Quinn, this is Rory, in case you haven't guessed."

He smiled. "I have. I'm quick that way." He was holding a gray horse by the reins but he dropped them to the ground and came over to offer his hand. "Good to meet you, Rory."

"Good to meet you, too, Quinn. But aren't you worried that horse will just walk away?"

"He's ground-tied."

"What's—" He caught himself before he'd revealed his ignorance.

Even so, Quinn gave him a sharp glance.

Damaris didn't seem to notice. She'd gone over to stroke the neck of the gray horse. "Is this dappled gray for me?"

"He is. This is Fifty Shades."

She laughed. "Of course he is. Pleased to meet you, handsome guy."

"He's on loan from Crimson Cliffs Ranch. So is the palomino April's riding. We pulled from every resource we had."

"I'm thrilled with this one. The genetics that produce such a color fascinate me." She glanced at the other two. One was the color of light suede with a black mane and tail. His lower legs were black, too, as if he had on socks. "I see you have Banjo saddled. Who's the third one? I don't recognize him."

"That's Diablo. Should be perfect for you, Rory."

"I'm sure he'll be fine." Diablo? That didn't sound good. Although the brown horse didn't look much like a devil with his head drooping and his eyes closed.

"Is Diablo from Crimson Cliffs, too?" Damaris looked him over. "I don't remember a Wild Creek horse with that name."

"He's ours. Kendra and I found him a few months ago. Whoever named him has a sense of humor. Nothing devilish about this animal. He's a sound fifteen-year-old with good manners."

Some of Rory's tension eased. He was on board with a sleepy horse who had good manners. Not even Diablo's tail twitched. It wasn't braided with ribbons, likely because he hadn't been meant to ride in the wedding.

Quinn picked up the gray horse's reins and glanced at Damaris. "Ready to mount up?"

"You betcha." She approached the horse from the left, handed her bouquet to Quinn and put her booted foot in the left stirrup. Good to know that was the side to use. She mounted swiftly, despite the extra material of the split skirt. After retrieving her bouquet and riding away from the hitching post, she spun her horse around, clearly waiting for him.

He was torn. He wanted her company on the trip to the meadow, but if she stayed to watch him get on this creature, she might figure out that he'd never been astride one in his life.

He gazed up at her. "You'd best be goin'. Catch up with the others. I'll be right behind you."

"I can wait. We'll make Ryker's fourteen-hundred hours, no problem."

"All right." He turned toward Quinn. "Let's do it."

The light of amusement in Quinn's gray eyes said it all. He knew he was dealing with a beginner. "Then allow me to introduce you to Diablo. I think you'll like him."

"I'm sure I will."

"He may not look like it now, but having a rider on his back puts a spring in his step. He'll make you look good."

"Does he ever rear up on his hind legs?"

"Not unless you want him to." Quinn lowered his voice. "You have zero experience, right?"

Denying it was stupid. This bloke wasn't the type you could fool. "How did you know?"

"Son, I've been around riders all my life. You don't fit the profile."

"But I want to."

"That's an admirable goal. If you stay open to it, there's much to be learned on the back of a horse. Here's the deal with Diablo. He moves out as if he's in a parade, but Kendra bought him because he's great with kids."

"It's a horse for wee bairns?" Now he could breathe easy.

"I had a hunch you might not be ready for a more spirited animal. Need a boost?"

"No, thank you. I can manage." He might not know what he was doing, but he could mount up with flair, like he'd seen in the movies.

Shoving his boot in the left stirrup, he pushed off with vigor. Too much vigor, it turned out. Somehow he overshot the saddle, lost his left stirrup in the process and was forced to slide to the ground on the far side of the blasted horse. The animal turned his head and gave him a long-suffering glance. Bloody hell.

3

Damaris gulped back her laughter. Rory wouldn't appreciate that kind of reaction, but God, he was funny. She still wasn't sure how he'd managed that stunt, but it would have made an awesome video. He might look and sound like Jamie Fraser, but he couldn't ride a lick.

He was enthusiastic, though. And strong. Vaulting clear over the horse required muscles.

His slight hesitation as they'd approached the horses had tipped her off that he might not be a seasoned horseman, but this crazy move branded him as a rank beginner. How he handled his epic fail would tell a lot about him.

He walked around the back of the horse, oblivious to the danger of getting kicked. Quinn opened his mouth to warn him, closed it again and shook his head. Chances were Diablo wasn't prone to kicking if Kendra and Quinn had made him part of the Wild Creek stable, but Rory had much to learn about safety.

Before trying to mount again, Rory turned and executed an elaborate bow in her direction. "I didn't judge that quite right."

"You'll do better this time."

"Can't do much worse." He climbed on with great care, swinging his leg slowly over Diablo's hindquarters, settling his firm buns in the saddle and his right foot in the stirrup. Then he heaved a sigh and glanced at Quinn. "That was the hard part, right?"

"I wouldn't say that, son. Let me give you a quick tutorial. Nudge him in the ribs to make him go. Pull back gently on the reins to make him stop. Laying the reins on the left side of his neck will make him turn right and vice versa."

Rory nodded. "That sounds simple enough."

"Sitting astride a two-thousand-pound animal is never simple. I'll be riding with you to make sure this goes well."

"If you want to go ahead and catch up with Kendra, I can coach him," Damaris said.

"Thanks for the offer, but since he's on a Wild Creek horse, ultimately he's Kendra's legal responsibility." Quinn mounted Banjo and looked over at her. "I'd better handle this. We'll be moving a little slower, but we'll be along shortly."

His subtle suggestion to head on out and let him give Rory his first riding lesson made sense. "Okey-doke. I'll see you later, Rory." She nudged Fifty Shades into a slow canter so she could catch up with the bridal party.

Maybe it was just as well if Quinn took charge of Rory for the duration of the ceremony. She was here to support April. Rory was a lovely distraction, but a distraction nevertheless.

Props to him for accepting his screw-up without trying to make excuses for it. She added strength of character to his other attributes. Getting to know Rory McGavin would be a treat.

She passed the buckboard and called out a greeting. A few other guests were bringing wagons, but most folks had worked out a horseback option.

The all-equine wedding had been Ryker's brainstorm. He'd become thoroughly committed to the ambitious plan after discovering no one had ever seen it done. When Quinn's three sons and his brother Brendan had volunteered to direct rider traffic, that had sealed the deal. It was shaping up to be an historic event.

The weather had cooperated and so had the wildflowers. Purple, gold and pink splashes of color decorated both sides of the trail out to the meadow. Damaris caught up to Mandy, who was riding Eeyore, the horse she'd had since childhood. She'd been a year behind Damaris in school, but a shared connection with Wild Creek Ranch and the McGavins had made them friends. They'd spent many happy hours together on these trails.

Mandy swiveled in her saddle. "Oh, good. I was hoping that was you coming up behind me. I need a favor. This kid is pressing on a very inconvenient spot. I'd just about decided to go behind a bush, but I hated to put down my bouquet. Eeyore might eat it."

"I'll hang onto him and your bouquet. There's a perfect spot over there. Might be the bush we used back in the day." She neck-reined Fifty Shades in the direction of a growth of tall, dense sagebrush.

Mandy followed behind. "Just like old times, right?"

"No kidding."

"You're a true friend, Damaris." She handed over her reins and bouquet before dismounting with a faint groan of discomfort. "Bet you don't have this kind of big fun in California."

"Nope. Haven't had to execute this maneuver in years."

"You need to keep in practice. You never know when you'll need such a valuable skill." She disappeared behind the sagebrush. "Where are Rory and Quinn?"

"Behind me somewhere, but they won't be along for a while. Scratch that. Here they come. They're moving faster than I expected."

"Why would they be going slow? They're not pregnant."

"No, but Rory's…getting acquainted with Diablo." No reason to spread the word that he knew zip about riding. Except an experienced rider would instantly recognize that he wasn't at home in the saddle. His posture was stiff and his heels were tilted up, not down.

He was holding the reins in a death grip, too, although his hand position was decent. Quinn would have taught him that much by now.

"Got a problem?" Quinn pulled up and Rory followed suit.

"Nothing we can't deal with," she called back.

Quinn nodded. "Gotcha." He touched the brim of his Stetson. "Let's go, Rory."

"Wait." Rory stayed where he was. "There's somethin' wrong or they wouldn't have stopped. We can't just leave."

"Yes, we can. They have it under control."

"But—"

"I'm answering nature's call, Rory!" Mandy's voice rang out clearly from behind the bushes.

"Ah." Rory grinned. "Thanks for tellin' me, lass. Didn't realize that kind of thing was done over here, too. We'll be off, then." He clucked to his horse and followed Quinn down the trail.

What a gorgeous man. Damaris sighed with pleasure. Was it her imagination or did he look more relaxed as he rode away? And sexier?

"Damaris?"

"Huh?" She glanced around.

"I'll take the reins and my bouquet, now."

"Sure." She transferred both. "We should get moving."

"Uh-huh." Mandy smiled. "Daydreaming a little, are we?"

"Some." She turned Fifty Shades around and started back down the trail. "It's the brogue. I got hooked on the *Outlander* books, and then the series came out on TV and—"

"Sam Heughan. I get it. My mom fell for him, too. She loves that series. The other day she asked if Zane and I had considered giving the baby a Scottish name to go with McGavin."

"That might be cool."

"It might. But instead of adding names, we need to pare down the two lists we already have."

"Is Damaris on the list?"

Mandy grinned. "No, I don't believe it is. Would you like it to be?"

"It has a nice ring to it, and I'd be..." She lost track of what she'd been about to say when the trail curved to provide a glimpse of the meadow. "Good Lord."

"That's impressive. Brendan and those Sawyer boys are actually pulling it off."

"The mounted guests look like an extremely large drill team."

"Don't they? I almost expect them to break into columns and do some maneuvers." Mandy stood in her stirrups. "I see Kendra and Quinn up front."

"And Rory." Damaris was tall enough to see without standing. "But where are Ryker and the groomsmen? Shouldn't they be lined up in front with the minister?"

"Zane was cryptic about their ultimate plan." Mandy checked her phone. "We still have five minutes before the magic hour. We'd better check in." She turned Eeyore and rode up a small rise to a nearby grove of trees. A clearing that was mostly shielded from the meadow had been designated as the gathering place for the bridal party.

When they rode in, April was standing in her stirrups peering through a gap in the trees. She glanced over at Damaris and Mandy. "Did you see any sign of Ryker and the rest of the guys?"

Damaris shook her head. "I figured you must know where they are."

"Not a clue."

"I'm sure they're here, somewhere." Kevin, April's dad, looked relaxed and serene. That had been his default setting all the years Damaris had known him. Slim and fit, he had the kindest face of anyone she knew.

"Yes, but where? It's almost time and he's the one who was so determined that it would start at—" She paused. "Is that thunder? Man, I hope we don't get rain after all."

"That's not thunder." Damaris turned toward the rumbling sound. "I think your dashing sweetheart and his band of brothers are coming to claim you."

April gasped. "Oh, my God, you're right. Look at those crazy guys!"

A line of riders, dark coats flapping and hands clamped to their black Stetsons galloped down a nearby hill with Ryker in the lead. They pulled up short on an imaginary line to the minister's left. Their horses pawed and snorted as each man took his assigned place.

Damaris consulted her phone and then held it up so everyone could see. "Fourteen-hundred hours! The man's precise."

April's smile was a thing of beauty. "And I love him for it. Guess it's high time I married that cowboy."

4

Horses, horses, everywhere. And a few wagons parked off to the side. Rory had traded an avalanche of names and faces for more ponies and horse-drawn wagons than he'd ever seen in one place except in the movies.

Quinn's decision to station himself next to Diablo was smart under the circumstances. If even one of these beasts took a notion to act up, the bonnie show could become a nightmare. Quinn's steady presence would guarantee Diablo wouldn't be that horse.

Rory had welcomed Quinn's instruction during his first horseback ride, which had turned out to be more of a challenge than he'd anticipated. He also welcomed Quinn's quiet commentary identifying the groomsmen lined up in front of them.

Ryker, the groom, was obvious. Quinn pointed out the other four cousins, distinctively different except that they all had Kendra's deep blue eyes. Zane was the second oldest, followed by the twins, Bryce and Trevor. They weren't identical twins, thank God, which would help identify them. Cody was the youngest.

That left the pilots—Badger, Ryker's best man, and Aaron, the fifth groomsman. Rory studied the faces, each shadowed by a black Stetson. He didn't have much confidence he'd retain everything Quinn had told him.

Still, it was kind of Quinn to help him out. Quinn and Damaris had a similar calming effect on him. Not identical, though. He had no desire to kiss Quinn.

Damaris was a different story. She had a mouth designed for lipstick adverts. Her lips might taste even better than they looked, but he wouldn't be finding out. Kissing had helped create the mess he'd left behind in Scotland.

His close call still made him shudder. Weddings were all well and good for others and this lusty ceremony was fine entertainment, but he enjoyed being single. If he knew what was good for him, he'd not be kissing any lasses while he was visiting his American cousins.

One of the twins—Bryce?—dismounted, walked over to the Wild Horse wagon and vaulted to the seat next to the driver. That was Jim. Faith's dad. Then Bryce leaned over the back of the seat, reached for the guitar one of the women handed him and began strumming a lovely melody. Professional quality playing, too.

The soft murmur of conversation stopped and everyone swiveled in their saddles to face the wide aisle between the rows of mounted guests. A group sigh arose as a man appeared walking beside a Shetland pony dripping in ribbons.

He kept one hand on the bridle and the other on a curly-headed blonde moppet sitting on the pony. She wore a crown of flowers, a frothy pink dress and sparkly shoes. No doubt she was Pax, Leigh's bairn.

Clutching a basket of rose petals, she sprinkled them carefully on the ground as she warbled along to the tune played by the guitarist. If Rory ever got married, he'd want a wee sprite like Pax leading the procession.

Once Pax and her daddy reached the end of the aisle, the parade of bridesmaids began. Rory envied the relaxed way the ladies rode with reins grasped loosely in one hand and a bouquet held in the other.

The first three down the aisle were the ones he hadn't sorted yet—Faith, Nicole and Olivia. He thought Faith might be the one with the long braid. She'd woven ribbons into it.

Ah, here came Mandy, the lass who was pregnant with his second cousin, the very same lass who took care of necessary business on the trail without fuss and feathers. He admired her for that.

His breath hitched as Damaris rode in next, a happy smile on her face. She was nicer to look at every time he saw her.

April's sister followed Damaris. Then Bryce ended the current tune and launched into an enthusiastic wedding march. April appeared, her golden horse led by a man who must be her father.

Rory barely recognized April. Earlier she'd seemed subdued, attractive in an understated way. Not anymore. Her joyful expression transformed her from mildly pleasing to stunningly beautiful. Her luminous gaze focused on her groom and she smiled.

Rory glanced at his formidable cousin. The muscular Air Force vet had ridden in looking fiercely determined. His broad shoulders and military bearing likely intimidated anyone who considered crossing him. But now...the man was awestruck.

On Rory's left, someone sniffed and he turned toward the sound. Tears dribbled down Aunt Kendra's cheeks as she kept her attention firmly on her eldest son and his stunned reaction. She couldn't have wiped away those tears if she'd wanted to. She held tight to Quinn's hand on one side and her friend Jo's on the other. Jo's face was shiny with tears, too.

During the ride to the meadow, Quinn had explained that Jo had been a second mother to Kendra's sons. She was the person who'd helped fill the gaping hole left when their father had died so young. Mandy had grown up with the McGavin brothers, and when she'd married Zane, the link between the two families had grown even stronger.

Since Quinn had fallen in love with Kendra, it seemed fitting that his brother was now crazy about Jo. Brendan anchored the end of the row and held tight to Jo's other hand. They were all intent on the ceremony, even though each of them sat on a sizeable animal and only Brendan and Rory had a grip on the reins of their respective horses. The others had looped the reins around the saddle horn.

Rory held his reins *and* the saddle horn for good measure. The movies made riding look easy but it wasn't. Judging from the level of expertise exhibited by this crowd, he was the least capable of the bunch, except for the non-riders in the buckboard. Good thing he hadn't chosen that mode of transportation. He wasn't used to being dead last in anything. If he intended to stick around Wild Creek Ranch, he had work to do.

But now wasn't the time to be worrying about it. He'd stumbled upon a major event in the life of these folks—the eldest McGavin pledging his troth to his lady love. The happy couple deserved his respectful attention.

He had a better view of April's face than Ryker's, but their words, spoken with conviction, were clear as a church bell. He had no doubt these two were soul mates, like his ma and da.

The action paused for another love song, this one performed by Bryce and one of the bridesmaids, a ginger lass who would look at home in a tartan. Was that Nicole? Maybe. He looked over at Damaris, the keeper of the spreadsheet.

She was completely into this, her gaze intent and her breathing shallow. Was she looking for her soul mate? Some smart bloke who understood those equations on her dressing gown?

Given a few minutes to examine them he could have identified most if not all. His chemistry degree had been of no use while slaving away in the distillery's warehouse, but he'd been promised that was only a starting point. That promise meant nothing now.

The ceremony continued with rings exchanged and vows given. The unobtrusive photographer managed to be in the exact right place at the perfect time. And then...it was over. Ryker and April leaned toward each other from the back of their respective horses and exchanged a sweet kiss. That was that.

Except not quite. As the kiss ended, Ryker slipped his arm around April's waist and effortlessly lifted her onto his horse. Her squeak of surprise confirmed they hadn't planned this in advance. But she laughed and wound her arms around his neck as he settled her across the saddle in front of him.

Wheeling his horse around, he cried out a jubilant *YES* and galloped down the aisle as the crowd cheered. Rory cheered right along with them. He hadn't officially met Ryker McGavin, but he'd already learned a lot about his cousin. He was intense and devoted. He had an amazing sense of style. And he was one hell of a rider.

Evidently he'd coordinated with his father-in-law because the guy stepped in immediately to take charge of April's mount. He moved the golden horse to one side as the bridal party and the groomsmen paired up to head down the aisle.

Rory turned the recessional into his own private guessing game. Badger was with Leigh, April's sister. Mandy was with Zane. Trevor was with...who? Wait, if the one with the braid was Faith, then the woman with Trevor was Olivia. For sure Damaris was not with a McGavin. She was with that Aaron bloke, the pilot, who rode as well as the rest of the men around here.

Bryce stayed to provide the getaway music. The ginger who might be Nicole stayed behind to sing with him. They behaved as if they were a couple. If only he could see that roster Damaris had drawn up. He just—

"Our turn to go," Quinn said. "If you think you can handle it, I'd like to ride with Kendra."

"I can handle it."

"Kendra and I will go first, then you, then Jo and Brendan. That way, you'll have experienced riders in front and behind. Diablo is a steady horse. You'll be fine."

"Absolutely." Excellent. While the couple ahead and the one behind enjoyed their own private conversations, he could practice what Quinn had taught him on the way to the ceremony. Heels down, shoulders relaxed, reins held loosely in his left hand, right hand resting on his thigh. So he could reach for his sword, if he had one.

Quinn had told him that was how mounting on the left got started. A soldier's sword was worn on the left so he could grasp it with his right, assuming he was right-handed. Mounting on the right would have been awkward.

By now he'd been in the saddle long enough to get a wee bit used to the sensation. And to enjoy it. Sitting astride a fine-stepping horse had a certain nobility about it. Diablo was a prancer. He picked up his feet nice and proper. Arched his neck, too.

On the way in Rory had been too intent on the process and Quinn's instruction to notice the scenery. This time he looked around. Bonnie wildflowers. A rushing creek that sparkled in the sunlight.

Through the trees on the far side something moved. Then a wee fawn, its coat still spotted, came to the bank and leaned down for a drink. Its mother appeared and lowered her head to the water.

One second the fawn's muzzle was in the water. The next the bank gave way and the fawn tumbled in, thrashing in the water, going down, going under...

Rory turned Diablo in the direction of the creek and dug his heels into the horse's flanks. Diablo lunged forward and Rory grabbed the saddle horn to keep from flying off. He bounced in the saddle, lost his hat and lost his stirrups. Any minute he expected to hit the dirt.

But he stayed on. Diablo skidded to a stop at the edge of the creek and somehow Rory kept from sailing over the horse's head. As he slid to the ground, hoof beats and shouting erupted behind him but he didn't glance back.

All his attention was on the fawn. Its mother had jumped in after it, but the current carried the baby faster than she could swim. Running along the bank, Rory got a few yards ahead of the fawn and leaped in.

The cold water took his breath away as he fought the current. Grasping a thick branch overhanging the water he worked his way toward the middle of the creek and searched for the fawn.

There. The current was bringing it straight toward him. The wee animal struggled to keep its nose above water.

With luck, he'd be able to grab it around the neck and hold it until someone came. The creek tried to dislodge him from the branch and he tightened his grip. The rough bark bit into his palm.

"I've got a rope, son!" Quinn's voice. "If you can grab that critter and lift it, I'll get a rope on it."

"Good plan! It's almost here!"

Then the nose went under. Bloody hell. It couldn't drown now. Not now.

The nose popped up again about a foot away. Holding the branch with every ounce of strength in his fingers, he stretched his arm out and clutched where the fawn's neck should be. Yes!

But the little creature was limp. Didn't weigh much, though, so he hooked his arm under its belly and hoisted it above the churning surface of the water. Quinn's rope sailed out and dropped over the fawn's head.

"Tighten it as best you can and we'll pull the critter out!" Quinn yelled.

"He may be dead already!"

"Maybe not! Just get yourself out."

He made sure the noose was snug and let go. Quinn and Brendan were knee-deep in the water gently pulling the limp little body to shore.

Going hand-over-hand on the branch, Rory approached the bank. Aunt Kendra and Jo began wading in.

"Don't get in too far, ladies! The current's fast!"

"We know!" Kendra drew closer. "Why do you think it's named Wild Creek?"

"It's wild, all right." Breathing hard, he moved slowly along the branch toward shore.

"Take my hand." Kendra held hers out.

"I might pull you in."

"You won't," Jo said. "I'm holding onto her. Take her hand."

He got his feet under him before he gripped Kendra's hand, her very strong hand. He'd never known a lass with that kind of strength. The two ladies hauled him up the slippery bank and onto firm ground.

"Thank you for that." He gulped in air and looked around, dreading what he'd see. "Where's the fawn?"

"Over there." Kendra pointed.

"It's getting up!"

Jo nodded. "Because Brendan just gave it CPR."

"He did *what*?"

"I know that sounds crazy, but when I glanced over there, that's what he was doing. Guess it worked."

"I'll be damned. And there's the doe, a few yards away. Why didn't she go after Brendan?"

"I think she understands he was helping her baby. Animals seem to know he means them no harm."

"That's incredible. I thought for sure that wee fawn was done for."

"It would have been without you." Kendra put her hands on her hips and glared at him. "I'm glad you saved it and we have a happy ending, but holy shit, Rory! You could have drowned trying to save that critter! What were you thinking?"

"Good question." He ran his hands through his dripping hair. "The simple answer is that I wasn't thinking at all. I just acted. I tend to do that. It's my curse. And my blessin'."

<u>5</u>

The commotion behind Damaris had convinced her that someone had an emergency. It might not involve Rory, but she wanted to know that for sure.

She wheeled her horse around and glanced at Aaron, her assigned groomsman. "I'm going back."

"I'm going with you."

A short, quick ride took them to the source of the commotion—five people dismounted, four of them wet to the knees and one soaked to the skin. Rory.

Damaris leaped from her horse and hurried over to where he stood with Kendra and Jo. "What's going on?"

His wavy red hair was the color of merlot and his nearly transparent shirt stuck to his broad shoulders and chest. "It's a long story, lass."

She turned to Kendra and Jo. "What the hell happened?"

Kendra sighed. "I'll say this. Rory's heart's in the right place. Because of his quick response, a days-old fawn will live to see another sunrise. It's trotted off with its mother and we're all happy about that. But I came *this close* to losing a nephew."

Rory shook his head. "I didn't take as big a chance as you—"

"Yes, you did." She turned to Damaris. "He jumped, fully clothed, into Wild Creek. It's at the height of snowmelt. The current is—"

"I know." Damaris's stomach hollowed out. "That's why you forbid us to go near it this time of year." She looked up at Rory. "She's not kidding. That creek is so dangerous right now."

"The fawn would have drowned."

"You could have, too."

His jaw tightened. "I canna stand by when an innocent creature is in trouble."

Oh, Rory. You might not be able to ride a horse but you have the instincts of a hero. "I get that you were worried about the fawn, but couldn't you have called for help instead of jumping in the creek?"

He shook his head. "It would have died for sure if I'd waited even one second. It almost did, anyway, except that Brendan gave it CPR."

"Are you kidding?" Aaron joined the group. "Brendan gave the fawn CPR?"

"Aye. I didn't see it, but Jo did."

"That's amazing. Awesome team effort." Aaron glanced at Damaris. "Right?"

"I'm glad the fawn didn't die." She turned to Rory. "But thinking of you in that creek...it really scares me."

"I'll not apologize for leapin' in to save that young creature." He drew a shaky breath. "I will apologize for causin' my relations to fear for my life."

"Hang on." Quinn walked over with Brendan right behind. "We don't want to miss the *I'm sorry* part of this episode."

Kendra gazed at him. "He's apologizing for scaring us to death, but not for jumping into the creek in the first place."

"I can't fault him for jumpin' in to save the fawn," Brendan said. "I'd have done the same."

Kendra dismissed that with a wave of her hand. "I'd expect it of you, Brendan. You're a wildlife expert. But Rory—"

"He did what any of us would have," Quinn said, "including you."

"But we all understand the risks. Rory just got here. He doesn't even know how to ride, let alone—"

"Aye, you're right." Rory ran his fingers through his wet hair, combing it back from his forehead. "Any one of you would have made a better job of it. I didn't understand the danger, like you said. Never imagined I would die tryin' to save that fawn."

Kendra pierced him with a look. "Would it have made a difference if you'd known the risk you were taking?"

He paused, then gave her a sheepish smile. "Nay."

Damaris swallowed. "Well, I'm very glad you didn't die."

He met her gaze. "Me, too, lass. Seems as though I might need a keeper while I'm here."

If that was a hint, she was taking it. "I'd be happy to handle that job." She maintained her cool on the outside, but inside she was turning cartwheels. Talk about a dream assignment.

"Then it's settled," Kendra said. "You couldn't ask for a more level-headed person to guide you than Damaris."

Level-headed? Her head didn't feel particularly level when she was staring into his blue eyes, but she'd do her best under challenging circumstances.

Kendra glanced around at the group. "Is everyone ready to continue the celebration?"

"I am." Rory pulled his wet shirt away from his chest. "But I'll need to change clothes."

"That goes for several of us," Kendra said.

"And I'll need my horse."

Quinn pointed to the brown gelding standing near the creek. "He's right where you left him."

"So he is. He must be ground-tied."

Quinn smiled. "In a manner of speaking."

"I'll fetch him." Rory's long strides covered the distance. Along the way he scooped up his hat and settled it on his head. He paused, then moved to Diablo's left side.

His mounting style wasn't smooth. He used the saddle horn and his wet jeans made a squishing sound as he plopped down on the saddle. But he laid the reins against the right side of the horse's neck and turned the gelding toward the trail with a show of confidence.

"He'll get there," Quinn said. "He's got heart."

"Of course he does." A gleam of pride lit Kendra's eyes. "He's a McGavin."

* * *

Everyone who'd taken part in the fawn rescue had changed into dry clothes, including Rory. In his jeans, plaid shirt and Western hat, he could almost pass for a Montana cowboy, except for his brogue.

Damaris wanted nothing more than to hang out with him, but she was a member of the wedding party and that meant posing for group pictures prior to the barbeque and then taking her assigned place during dinner. Two picnic tables had been pushed together to form a head table, but guests could sit wherever they wanted.

Soon after Rory had come out of the house after changing clothes, the McGavin boys had gathered around to welcome him to the family amid much handshaking and backslapping. Then Caitlin summoned everyone in the wedding party to gather for pictures. Damaris was swept into that group.

"I'll check with you later," she called out to Rory as she followed the group to the spot Caitlin had chosen.

"No problem." He gave her a smile. "I'll be fine on my own."

Clearly he was. By the time Caitlin was finished, Rory was in an animated discussion with Ellie Mae Stockton, the eighty-something clerk from Pills and Pop. The fifties-themed drugstore was closed for the day, as were most of the businesses in Eagles Nest.

Since Rory seemed to be doing fine, Damaris took her seat at the head table. Next time she checked on Rory's whereabouts, he was seated at a table with Ellie Mae and Tansy Emerson, a bartender at the Guzzling Grizzly. The town's most famous establishment was also closed today. Soon they were joined by Ellen and Jenny, servers at the GG.

Rory's popularity made Damaris smile. It figured that he'd attract women of all ages with those blue eyes and winning smile. The tale of his fawn rescue had likely spread through the crowd by now, increasing his appeal. Add in his charming accent and it was no wonder he was surrounded.

Once the guests were all seated, the Sawyer boys brought bottles of champagne and sparkling water to each table. Glasses were filled and the guests gazed expectantly at Badger Calhoun, Ryker's best man.

Badger lounged in his chair as if unaware all eyes were on him. Then he sat up straighter and gazed out at the crowd. "Why're y'all starin' at me?" Then he smacked his forehead. "That's what I forgot to do! Write my toast!"

Several people grinned. Even Damaris, who had only known Badger a few days, didn't believe for a minute he'd forgotten.

He stood slowly and picked up his champagne flute. "Guess I'll have to wing it. A little flyboy humor, folks."

Ryker groaned. "Here we go."

"Now, that's a fact." Badger turned to him. "Here we go, especially you, Cowboy. For anyone who doesn't know, Cowboy is the nickname we gave him when we were in the service. We even went to a flea market when we were on leave and bought him this." Reaching under the table, he pulled out a battered straw cowboy hat.

"Hey!" Ryker tried to grab it. "Did you steal that out of my cockpit?"

"I did." Badger held it out of reach. "Leave it be. It's a prop for my speech."

"Thought you didn't have a speech."

"Turns out I do. And this is it. You and April have somethin' very special. You two are stuffed to the gills with love, more than enough for a lifetime together. You're a lucky man, Cowboy."

Ryker's voice was gruff with emotion as he turned to April and squeezed her hand. "Yes, I am."

"Yes, sir." Badger nodded. "As my granny used to say, you're luckier than a bear in a patch of raspberries. But I'm not goin' to claim all your luck is on account of this hat."

"That's a relief," Ryker said, "because I—"

"However, I would suggest you expand its use."

"Oh?"

"Instead of keepin' it in the cockpit all the damn time, take it home at night. Hang it on the back of a kitchen chair, or better yet, on the bedpost. Use it as a reminder every wakin' moment that you're one lucky bastard to have a woman like April sharin' your life."

Ryker cleared his throat and stood. "I will, Badger. Great idea. Thank you." He embraced his friend. "Now give me the hat."

"Glad to."

Taking off his pristine black Stetson, Ryker put on the battered straw hat, turned to April and pulled her to her feet. "April, would you be willing to kiss a man wearing something this mangy?"

She tilted it back and stood on her tiptoes. "I'd be honored, Cowboy."

As they kissed, Badger led the applause and Damaris clapped until her hands stung.

"To my best friend Cowboy and his beautiful bride April!" Badger lifted his glass and drained it.

April and Ryker linked arms and sipped their champagne. Damaris followed their example instead of Badger's and took only a small amount of the bubbly. With a handsome Scot under her care, she needed to keep her wits about her.

The meal was served by kids from the ENHS home economics department. When the band started tuning up over by the elevated wooden dance platform, Damaris excused herself from the head table and headed for Rory.

She wanted to talk with him before he was swept onto the dance floor by his admirers. She'd offered the knowledge from her spreadsheet and now might be a good time to share it with him.

She approached the table. "Can I borrow Rory for a minute?"

Rory stood up immediately. "Aye, Damaris. I've wanted to—"

"If you take him away from us," Ellie Mae said, "promise you'll try to get an answer to our burning question."

Oh, boy. She had a good idea what it was.

"He refuses to give us a simple yes or no," Ellie Mae continued. "Our question is about kilts. Do you know what question I mean?"

"I believe I do."

"Oh, and FYI, we've confirmed that Rory brought his kilt and his plaid, which is that thing they wrap around their chest."

"I know what it is." Rory had those items in his suitcase? What fun if he'd dress as a Highlander while he was here. She glanced around the group. "Have any of you seen *Outlander*?" She was met with head shakes and blank looks. "You're missing a great series. Besides, it would answer your question."

"I've heard of it." Tansy combed her fuchsia hair behind her ears. "Isn't it historical?"

"The heroine goes back in time to Scotland in 1743, so yes, most of it is set in the past."

Ellie Mae waved her hand. "We don't care what Scotsmen did back in the day. We're just curious as to what they do *now*."

"Have you looked it up online?"

"That's no fun," Ellie Mae said. "We have a native Scotsman here, in the flesh. Can't get more authentic info than that."

Damaris glanced at Rory. "Is it a deep dark secret?"

His blue eyes sparkled with mischief. "Aye."

"That's it, then, Ellie Mae. You can't expect a Highlander to reveal the secrets of his clan, now, can you?"

She sighed. "Well, when you put it that way, I suppose not, especially to casual acquaintances. Never mind. We all have so few deep dark secrets left. Keep yours while you can, Rory."

"I intend to, Ellie Mae." He looked at Damaris. "Where to, lass?"

"Let's go sit by the fire."

"Brilliant."

"Alrighty, then." She chose a bench near the fire but not too close. "How's this?"

"Perfect. Just now I was talkin' with people I'm not related to, which was more relaxin', but I want to be able to greet my relations by name. Am I right that the ginger with the long curly hair is Nicole?"

"Yes." She brought up her spreadsheet on her phone. "Here's Nicole, along with a picture of her performing with Bryce. They're making a name for themselves in country music."

"That explains why they sound so good."

"They're booking gigs all over the country, but they still play at the Guzzling Grizzly a lot. Bryce co-owns it with Michael Murphy, who's right over there." She pointed to a tall guy several yards away.

"Have I met him?"

"Not yet. That woman next to him, the one with the long, dark hair, is Roxanne, Quinn's daughter." She scrolled through her spreadsheet. "Here's the breakdown for the Sawyer family."

He cupped his hand around hers and peered at her phone. "Is Roxanne the artistic one who braided the manes and tails?"

"Uh-huh." His warm hand cradling hers sent little squiggles of excitement up her arm. "See, you're getting it."

"It's a slow slog. Like pourin' honey from a crock." His breath tickled her cheek as he shifted his weight on the bench.

Hip-to-hip, they were generating heat from the point of contact. Was it affecting him? He didn't act like it. She refreshed her screen. "Let's go through the list and see how many people you can identify. I'll bet it's more than you think."

"All right. Let's start with the McGavins. Kendra, no problem. Same with Ryker and April. I recognize Zane, now, but I don't know much about him."

"He's Kendra's right-hand-man at the ranch and he's married to Mandy."

"Ah, Mandy. I'll not be forgettin' her."

"Zane also created Raptors Rise, a birds of prey rescue organization."

"Now that excites me. Which birds of prey?"

"Eagles, mostly goldens but some bald eagles, plus hawks and owls."

"We have goldens in Scotland. The birds of prey have a rough go in the UK like they seem to have here. Where's his operation located?"

"Right down the road. I could take you over there sometime in the next few days."

"You'll still be here?"

"Kendra invited me to stay on after the wedding is over. I'll be around through next weekend." *The better to see you in your kilt and plaid, laddie.*

"That lowers my stress level a wee bit. For all I knew, you were leavin' tomorrow."

"I considered it, but I can use the R and R." She glanced at him. "Do you have a timeframe for your visit?"

"Not exactly."

"So you haven't booked a return flight?"

"Not yet."

She hesitated. Oh, what the heck. "Your visit seems very...spontaneous."

"Because it is."

"You told Kendra that you took a notion and hopped on a plane. Do you do that a lot?"

"Never."

"Then why now?"

"It was a good time to leave."

"I guess you must be between jobs, then."

"Aye." He grimaced. "And...it's best if I'm not in Scotland right now."

That certainly was cryptic. "Are you running from something?"

He exhaled and lowered his head. "That I am, lass."

<u>6</u>

Rory was glad Damaris had asked. On the plane coming over, he'd debated whether to make a clean breast of things to Kendra once the dust had settled from his arrival. Seemed only fair to let her know this wasn't strictly a pleasure trip.

That issue had become a moot point. She'd had no time to listen to such nonsense and it would have been entirely inappropriate, anyway. Rescuing the fawn in the middle of the wedding celebration was more than enough distracting behavior on his part without burdening her with his tale of woe.

Since Damaris had volunteered to keep track of him, maybe she was the logical one to tell, anyway. She could advise him on how to handle his delicate situation. She seemed to fancy him, although revealing his primary reason for this visit might alter her good opinion.

He'd take that chance because telling her would be a relief. He drew in a breath and let it out slowly, the way she'd suggested earlier today. "The truth is, I made a colossal mistake. I took the wrong woman to bed."

Her brows snapped together. "She was married?"

"No. For all my faults, I draw the line at that."

"Then why was she the wrong woman?"

"She's the only daughter of the man who owns the large distillery where I work. *Worked.* I'll not be goin' back there."

Damaris groaned. "The boss's daughter. That's a recipe for disaster."

"I resisted her for weeks, but she was determined."

"Wait. *She* seduced *you*?"

"She did." He looked over at Damaris. "I have a weakness when it comes to a bonnie lass." Especially one with a mouth like ripe cherries. Damaris had such a mouth. Kissing her would be—

"I'm confused, Rory. If she wanted to have sex with you, why are you in trouble?"

"First of all, because she was a virgin. I didn't know until it was too late."

"That doesn't change the fact that it was her idea to—"

"Second of all, she thought that since I'd claimed her virginity, we must marry."

"That's archaic!"

"I told her so. I also said I didn't love her."

"And?"

"She didn't care. She wanted me and was convinced I'd come to love her once we were married. She promised me swift advancement in her father's distillery. I'd finally be able to use my chemistry degree instead of slavin' away in the warehouse on the night shift."

"Sounds tempting."

"Aye, if you're willin' to sell your soul."

She met his gaze and her mouth tilted at the corners. Her kissable mouth. "Well, there's that."

"Anyway, she said her da would ruin my future in the distillery business if I didn't go along with her grand plan. On top of that, her three brothers would batter me somethin' terrible if they ever caught me alone on some dark night. I could handle the beatin'. It's the suspense of not knowing when it would happen that I'd hate."

"Isn't that kind of threat illegal?"

"It is, and my brother Aleck—he's a solicitor—wanted me to bring charges against her."

"And why not bring charges if you have a brother who would take care of the legal part for you?"

"Didn't seem like a gentlemanly way to handle it, bringin' charges, embarrassin' everyone. Better to make myself scarce for a while."

"She's lucky you're a nice guy. How long do you think it'll take before you can go back?"

"Not long, I hope. If I'm lucky, she'll latch onto another Prince Harry lookalike who's only too willin' to marry her and become a part of her wealthy family."

"Prince Harry?" She couldn't see it. Sam Heughan from *Outlander*? Definitely.

"It's my ginger hair. Catriona reads everythin' she can find about the royals and she'd love to be part of that world. Guess I look enough like Prince Harry that I satisfied at least part of her fantasy."

"That's some story. The good news is that it motivated you to visit your relatives."

"I don't want them to think that's the *only* reason, though. I've always dreamed of makin' the trip."

"And what do you think so far?"

He gazed into her green eyes. "It's goin' to be an adventure."

"Is that a good thing?"

"A very good thing. I'm thirsty for adventure. Even though I'm worn to the nubs, I—"

"Of course you are. You've traveled halfway around the world, ridden a horse for the first time and leaped into an icy creek to save a fawn. Maybe you should call it a night. I'm sure everyone would understand."

"Call it a night? When there's a party goin' on? I'm a bit tired, but I've never felt more alive. The band's soundin' fine. Fancy a turn around the floor with me?"

"Oh!" She seemed startled. "I don't—"

"I'm a fair dancer. I promise not to step on your wee feet."

"My feet aren't wee and I'm more likely to step on yours. I haven't danced in...I can't remember the last time. And I wasn't very good at it then, either. You might want to ask someone else."

He smiled.

"What?"

"Didn't you see me vault clear over that beast today?"

"Well, yes, but—"

"You can't do worse than that. I expect you'll do much better." He stood and held out his hand. "Gather your courage and dance with me, lass."

"You asked for it." She put her hand in his and stood. "Can you dance the two-step?"

"Is that what you call what they're doin'?"

"Uh-huh."

"Different from the two-step I know, but I'll give it a try. Let me watch for a bit." He paused at the edge of the wooden platform and studied the movements of the dancers. "I believe I've got it. Let's go."

"That didn't take you long."

"I love to dance." He led her up the steps. "Always have." Tucking her in close, he spun them into the whirling dancers. Immediately his feet tangled with hers and he was forced to stop.

Her face turned pink. "See? I warned you."

"Easy does it. We'll get this." He wanted to more than ever after holding her for those few seconds. She felt *so* good in his arms. Warm and soft. "Let's leave the platform for a bit." He guided her back down the steps.

At the bottom, she turned to him. "Look, now that you know I'm not very good, you don't have to dance with me just because you asked. I'll bet Tansy Emerson is a much better—"

"Hey, hey. None of that. Come over here where we have a good view of the footwork."

"That won't help."

"It might. Why do you have equations on your dressin' gown?"

She stared at him.

"Bear with me. Are you a scientist?"

"Theoretical physicist."

He nodded. "Thought it might be somethin' like that. I don't know that field well, but I'll take a guess that sometimes you study patterns."

"I do."

"Then just find the pattern in the footwork. And then the complimentary pattern."

"Oh, I can do that just fine. I can analyze the movements from all angles and have it down cold. But in the heat of the moment, I—"

"Performance anxiety?"

She took a deep breath. "Partly. I've never been talented at dancing, so I anticipate screwing up and sure enough, I do."

"I have an idea for fixin' that problem. Come with me." Taking her hand, he led her away from the barbeque area to a shadowy spot where they'd still be able to hear the music. "We'll dance here. No one can see if we stumble."

"I can't imagine how that will be any fun for you, dancing on the grass. The wooden floor is way better."

"I can dance anywhere. Let's try it." He coaxed her into his arms.

Her breath hitched as he started to move. "I really think this is—"

"Relax and visualize the pattern."

She stumbled against him and swore softly. "I'm hopeless, Rory. Give it up."

He should have agreed with her. Should have let her go. But her curvy body fit so perfectly against his. Instead of releasing her, he pulled her closer.

Her breathing was unsteady as she gazed up at him.

Even with her face in shadow, the wine-red lipstick she wore stood out. It was still perfect, as if she'd just applied it. Must be the kind that stayed on no matter what.

She swallowed. "I thought we came out here to dance."

"I swear that's all I meant to do."

"We're not dancing."

He took a shaky breath. "Strictly speakin' we're not."

"Then what are we doing, strictly speaking?"

"The truth is, I'm tryin' very hard not to kiss you."

Her breath caught. "You want to?"

"I've wanted to since I first laid eyes on you, lass. Your mouth is the perfect shape for kissin'."

"It is?"

"Didn't anyone ever tell you?"

"No."

"Well, it is." He brushed his thumb over her silken lower lip. "Been temptin' me for hours. But I don't need to be kissin' anyone."

"I wouldn't mind."

"You wouldn't?"

She slid her hands up his chest. "It would be an adventure. I've never kissed a Scotsman before."

"I've never kissed an American lass before, either." He leaned a little closer.

"Do you suppose we'd notice a difference?"

"I doubt it."

She pushed up on her toes, putting herself within range. "Let's test it and see."

"Good idea." Closing his eyes, he completed the journey, touching down on her ripe mouth with a groan of pleasure. What a treat to savor the plump curve of her lower lip and the perfect bow above it.

Raising his head a bit, he traced the outline of her mouth with his tongue before going back for more. He delved deeper, sipping and tasting as she gradually relaxed in his arms.

Then he lifted his lips away, just a wee bit, so he could whisper his request. "Dance with me."

Her answering sigh stirred his loins, but he resisted the urge to return to that seductive mouth. The band launched into a new tune and he moved in time with the drummer's rhythmic beat.

She followed. He tried a gentle turn, breaking the dance into slower, more measured steps. She stayed with him. He picked up the pace and she didn't falter.

A shaft of moonlight bathed her face. She was smiling.

He smiled back. "Havin' fun?"

She nodded.

"Want to go back?"

"No."

"Me, either." He whirled her around the grassy space and she didn't miss a step. When he spun her under his arm, she executed the maneuver like a pro, so he spun her the other way.

Her soft laughter spilled over him, a deluge of happiness. "I'm dancing."

"That you are, lass. And makin' a fine job of it." He'd shared the dance floor with dozens of partners, but none of them had filled him with more joy than Damaris.

As the tune ended, he twirled her once more, pulled her in and lowered his head for one more kiss. Just one.

With a soft whimper, she leaned into him.

Ah, lassie. He savored the press of her warm body and the softness of her lips a moment more before reluctantly lifting his head and taking a breath. "Enough."

"Says who?"

He chuckled. "Kissin' you is a pure delight. But I dropped out of the sky and landed in the middle of Ryker's weddin'. That's disruption enough without...without...."

"Front and center! Time for cake!" Ryker's commanding voice drew everyone's attention.

Rory gazed at Damaris. "That means us."

"Uh-huh."

"We should go." He offered his hand as they started back. "Do you like cake?"

"Not as much as I like kissing you."

He choked on a laugh and had to clear his throat before he could respond to that. "It appears I started somethin'."

"It appears you did." She glanced up at him. "What are you going to do about it?"

"That's a very good question." He had no bloody idea.

"Let me know if an answer occurs to you." She squeezed his hand, slipped hers free and hurried over to the head table to join the rest of the wedding party.

7

Damaris wasn't good at flirting or playing romantic cat and mouse games. Never had been. As she sat at the head table eating the best chocolate cake she'd ever tasted, she chatted with old friends and the new ones she'd made since arriving a couple of days ago. She didn't search the crowd for Rory's whereabouts. They could both use a little time to think.

He'd been the one to suggest dancing in the shadows, the one to admit he wanted to kiss her, although dancing in the shadows had given her that idea, too. Turned out he was a great kisser. If they'd been interrupted by Ryker's call to action, so be it.

She pointed a fork at her half-eaten slice of cake. "This is incredible. I haven't taken the time to stop at Pie in the Sky, but now I definitely will."

"Abigail and Ingrid do a stupendous job." Mandy scraped up the last crumbs. "If I weren't on my best behavior, I'd lick the plate."

Zane leaned closer. "Go ahead. I dare you."

"Nah. I'll just plan a visit there soon. The specialty coffees are good, too. You know what, Damaris? We should go there next week."

"If you have time, I'd love to. I'm on vacation but you're not."

"I have time. I'm ahead of schedule on clothing orders. April and I talked about having me make the dresses for this, but the vintage pattern with the split riding skirt was going to be super complicated so I bailed."

"It would have been too much to ask." April got up and came over to join the conversation. "Did I hear you two making a coffee date for next week? Now I'm jealous."

Mandy laughed. "Then by all means cancel your fabulous San Francisco honeymoon so you can hang out with us next week. I would if I were you."

"I would, too," Faith said. "Coffee dates are way fun. Can I horn in?"

"Only if you bring Noel," Mandy said. "Hey, Nicole and Olivia, want to do coffee next week, say Wednesday afternoon about two?"

"I'll be there," Nicole said. "Coffee dates are a special treat now that I've left Shear Delight."

April glanced at her. "Do you miss doing hair?"

"A little, but it was too crazy, performing regularly and putting in full days at the salon. Olivia, can you make it now that tax season's over?"

Oliva looked up from her phone. "Just checked my schedule. I can come."

"I have another great plan," Mandy said. "Besides the coffee date, let's do a movie night at my house next week. Thursday would be good."

Zane stood. "I think that's my cue to suggest Cody should host a guy's poker night at the A-frame on Thursday night."

"Do you see that?" April turned to Ryker. "They're making their plans right in front of us."

"I do see that."

"We have no choice," Mandy said. "We have to grab Damaris while she's in town and before our Scottish visitor monopolizes all her time."

"Right!" April walked over and put a hand on Damaris's shoulder. "What was that dancing in the dark routine all about, chica?"

She glanced up and smiled. "No clue. You'll have to find him and ask him."

"She doesn't have time," Mandy said. "She still has to pack."

April groaned. "Don't remind me. We can't stay much longer."

"So true," Ryker said. "Let's go have one last dance, though."

"You've got it, bridegroom." They headed over to the dance platform.

"Then I'm nominating myself to search out our bonnie Scotsman." Mandy pushed aside her plate and winked at Damaris. "See what he has to say for himself."

Damaris laughed. "I was kidding. I've got this."

"Good thing you two sorted that out," Nicole said. "Here he comes."

"You are so right." With a shiver of anticipation, Damaris left the table and met Rory before he reached it. "You look like a man with something on his mind."

"That's a fact." He met her gaze and lowered his voice. "Been thinkin' about those kisses."

"Me, too. Still am." And it was making her short of breath.

"The thing is, you'll only be here a week and I might not be stayin' much longer."

"True."

"I'll return to Scotland and you'll go back to California. We'll be thousands of miles apart."

"Also true."

"Logically, whatever happened could only be a...temporary diversion."

"Are you opposed to that?"

He hesitated.

"Because I'm not." That outrageous, so unlike her statement had popped right out, but now that she'd said it, she didn't want to take it back.

"You're not?"

She glanced around. Not the best venue to be talking about such intimate matters. "My contacts are bothering me. I need to go inside and get my glasses. Want to come with me?"

"I do." He fell into step beside her as she walked toward the ranch house. "I wondered if you wore contacts."

"Why?"

"When I first met you, you were squintin' as if you couldn't see clearly."

"That's an understatement. If I don't have my glasses or my contacts, I'm blind as a...I started to say bat, but I need to ditch that expression. Bats aren't blind."

"They use echolocation."

"They do. I'm fond of bats."

"Same here. Amazin' little creatures. Thought of goin' into wildlife management."

"Why didn't you?"

"It can break your heart. Mine, anyway. Makin' Scotch is fun, and it's a time-honored tradition in my country." He climbed the porch steps with her and lengthened his stride so he could open the front door.

"Thank you." Laughter and cheerful female conversation poured from the kitchen.

"Hey, Quinn," Kendra called out. "If that's you, we're almost out of ice. If you'd bring over what we stashed at your house, that would be—"

"It's not Quinn," Damaris called back. "I came in to swap my contacts for my glasses."

"Oh." Kendra walked out of the kitchen. "I tried texting him, but—hi, Rory."

"Hi. Want me to go tell him about the ice?"

"Sure, that would be great."

"Wait a sec." Damaris hurried toward her bedroom. "Let me grab my glasses and I'll go back out with you." So much for a quiet conversation with no potential eavesdroppers.

"I'll be here."

"Thanks." She quickly popped out her contacts and put on her glasses before going back to the living room. "There. Do I look smarter?"

He laughed. "Aye, but Kendra already told me you were very smart. Valedictorian of your class."

"She did, huh?" She walked with him out to the porch. "Was that before or after you kissed me?"

"Before. Right after I arrived."

"And you kissed me anyway?"

"Why not?"

"Some guys would wonder if I'm smarter than they are and decide against it."

"I don't wonder. I know you are. A theoretical physicist is way above my pay grade. Doesn't mean I don't want to kiss you."

"So what do you say to a temporary diversion?"

"You're serious about this, aren't you?"

"No, I'm *not* serious. That's the whole point. My life is nothing *but* serious. My area is dark matter, and you don't get much more obscure and hypothetical than that." She scanned the crowd. "There's Quinn in deep conversation with Ryker and April."

"I see them."

She started in that direction. "Let's relay the message, but let's offer to get the ice ourselves. I hate to pull him away now, when April and Ryker will be leaving pretty soon."

"Then I'll get the ice so you can stay until April and Ryker leave. I have my rental."

"But you won't know where you're going. I've spent plenty of quality time with April since I got here. I'm good. But Quinn's been knocking himself out getting ready for this, arranging horses for those who needed them and figuring out where to put all of them during the celebration. He hasn't had much time to talk with the bride and groom."

"Where *did* he put all those ponies?"

"They're out in the pasture. The saddles and bridles are lined up on the top rail of the corral. See?"

"They sure are. I didn't notice that before."

"A few are already gone because guests are starting to leave. They just walk to the corral, get their tack and locate their horses. If they need help, they just get one of the Sawyer boys to go down to the corral with them."

"Hard for me to imagine."

"I suppose it is. You didn't grow up like I did. Kendra taught me to ride when I was eight and I was out here every chance I could get, mostly with April and Mandy." She waved to Quinn. "We have a message from Kendra!"

"Oh, yeah?" He thumbed back his Stetson. "What's she need?"

"Ice, but Rory and I will get it. I know where it is and Rory has a rental car."

Quinn's lips twitched with the hint of a smile. "Sounds good."

"We'll probably be gone by the time you get back." April gave her a hug.

"Have a fabulous time." Damaris hugged Ryker goodbye, too. "You'll love San Francisco. Call me when you get home."

"I will." April gave her one more hug. "I know you're crazy busy with your project, but if you can possibly make another trip over, I'd love to see you."

"I'll do my best."

April turned to Rory. "Will you be here when we get back from our trip?"

"I very well might be."

"I hope so."

Ryker extended his hand. "That goes for me, too, cuz. We didn't get much time together, but if you're here when we get back, I'll take you up in the Beechcraft."

"I'd like that."

"We're gonna have to go," Damaris said. "Don't want to have an ice crisis." She glanced at Quinn. "Is the house open?"

"Yes, ma'am."

"We'll be off then." She blew a kiss to April and Ryker before starting toward the parking area.

Rory kept pace with her. "You act like you know where you're going."

"I do."

"How can you know which car is my rental?"

She grinned and swept a hand toward the row of pickups and SUVs. His tiny rental was half the size of every other vehicle there. "It's not hard."

"I see what you mean." He fished the keys out of his jeans pocket. "Quinn doesn't lock his house?"

"Most people don't around here."

He clicked the locks open on the rental. "Or vehicles?"

"Not usually."

"I'll have to tell ma and da that. They warned me to be sure and lock everything while I was in America. We don't do it so much back home, either, but they thought it was different here."

"Depends on where you live. In California, I lock up. I had to get used to it after Eagles Nest, where people tend not to worry about theft." She glanced at him. "Do you want me to drive?"

"No, I will."

"Then you need to get in on the other side."

He looked disoriented for a second. Then he flashed her a smile. "I thought I'd just open your door for you, lass."

"Nice save."

He frowned. "Excuse me?"

What an adorable guy. "It means you salvaged a moment that was actually a screw up."

"Oh." His expression turned sheepish. "I'm still not used to the steerin' wheel bein' over there."

"No wonder. You've only driven that way once in your life. I'd be happy to drive."

"Thanks, but I need to get used to it." He opened her door with a flourish. "And since I'm here..." He gestured toward the passenger seat.

"Thank you." She paused before getting in, stood on tiptoe and gave him a quick kiss on the mouth. Mm. Nice.

He blinked. "Was that for opening your door?"

"Nope. That was so you don't lose track of the subject we were discussing before we volunteered for this ice run."

<u>**8**</u>

Rory was in no mental shape to decide whether it was against his principles to begin an affair with Damaris, but it seemed he'd have to decide, anyway. It wasn't the sort of thing you asked to take a rain check on. Or be allowed to sleep on before voting aye or nay.

That would be insulting to Damaris. Only one answer was appropriate when a beautiful, intelligent woman, not to mention soft and cuddly, made such an offer. That offer had come out of the most tempting mouth he'd encountered since starting his kissing career. The answer had to be yes, and hell, yes.

On the drive to Quinn's house, she made her pitch. "I have a very demanding job. There's fierce competition among the scientists. Who's going to get that breakthrough? Who's going to identify that illusive particle that will win them a place in scientific history?"

"My money's on you, lass."

"My parents say so, too."

"Do they put pressure on you?" Despite the urgency of getting ice reinforcements, he took the dirt road to the highway slowly. The headlamps revealed the same ruts he'd encountered earlier and he did his best to avoid them.

"They don't. They just think I'm awesome."

"Are they scientists, too?" He gripped the wheel of the wee vehicle, which shimmied when he accidentally hit a rut. Having Damaris along was comforting, though it meant his hat had to go on the dash. But the cramped space brought him closer to Damaris.

"No, they're in real estate. They don't totally understand what my research is about, but they're convinced someday I'll win the Nobel Prize."

"That's touchin'." He stopped at the main highway and turned to her. "Would you like to win it?"

"Who wouldn't? But mostly it would be fun because they'd be so happy for me." She looked left and right. "There's no traffic. You can pull out. Go left and take the first road on your right."

He followed her directions and was once again on a bumpy dirt road that required sharp eyes and a firm grip on the wheel. "I'm guessin' you love your work."

"I do. I can't imagine anything better. It's just recently I've been stymied with my current project. It's a good time to take a break. I don't do that often."

"How often?"

"This trip is my first real vacation in...I'd say four years."

"Four *years*?"

"It might be closer to five. I'd have to figure it out. Let's see…I went to Disneyland with friends from the department the last time I took time off. You know what? It has been five years."

"What about dating?"

"You're kidding, right? I'm the most boring date you can imagine. I don't have time to keep up with pop culture or current events. Not many men want to talk about dark matter over dinner."

"I would."

"Thank you, but that's just it. I don't want to talk about dark matter, because it's all I think about at work. I want to talk about something else, but I don't have a store of amusing anecdotes or a treasure trove of amazing facts."

"You know about bats."

"A little. Not enough to take me through a dinner date."

"You know how to ride."

"Now that is true. But you can't imagine how few people care. It sucks as a conversational topic. I say *guess what? I know how to ride a horse!* And they say *that's nice* and that's the end of it."

"I care that you're a good rider. You have a skill I want to learn."

"I'd be happy to teach you. I don't have a whole lot to do this week, which isn't true of everybody else around here."

"I'll take you up on that offer." He took a deep breath. "And the other one, too."

"Oh, yeah?"

"Gladly. Any man would count himself lucky to be invited into your bed."

"It's gallant of you to say so." She sounded breathless.

"It's the truth." His breathing wasn't all that steady, either.

"We, um, need to consider where this bedding will take place. If Kendra and Quinn are staying at Wild Creek Ranch, I wouldn't feel comfortable getting jiggy in one of the bedrooms."

"Good." He hadn't heard the term *jiggy* before but in context he could figure it out. "I wouldn't, either."

"Sometimes she spends the night at Quinn's though."

"That would help."

"How do you feel about doing it outside?"

"A possibility." The more they discussed it, the more he was willing to do it in a broom closet.

"Do we have a plan, then?"

"Seems as if we do." And he had a wee problem going on below his belt because of this topic. He barely had enough room in the driver's seat with the seat pushed back as far as it would go. Crunched as he was, arousal made it worse.

He cleared his throat. "I should mention that I'm ill-prepared for this adventure we've been talkin' about. I'll need to visit the pharmacy tomorrow."

"Pills and Pop. You'll have to check the hours because not everything is open on Sunday."

"I'll look it up on my phone."

"Ellie Mae works at Pills and Pop. Did she tell you?"

"No. She was more interested in finding out whether a Scotsman wears anythin' under his kilt."

"You're liable to get that question a lot. Many American women are fixated on the idea of a Scotsman going commando under his kilt."

"Evidently. The thing is, there's no definitive answer." The topic of kilts had helped calm his tadger. "Everybody chooses differently. But Ellie Mae wasn't satisfied with that answer."

"I'm sure she wasn't. She's a pistol." The outline of a low-slung ranch house appeared at the end of the road. Lights shone from the porch and through one of the front windows. "We're here."

"Where should I park?"

"In front of the house is fine."

He parked the rental, shut off the headlamps and opened his door. Then he managed to extricate himself without groaning out loud. By the time he'd retrieved his hat from the dash and joined her on the wide front porch, his jeans no longer pinched so bad.

He probably didn't need the hat right now, but he loved wearing it. Settling it on his head, he waited as she opened the front door. Opening it for her made no sense in this case, but he was getting confused about protocol.

Might as well ask. "I have a question about doors."

She paused and looked back at him. "Like this one?"

"Well, not really, because you're in charge of this operation so I'd expect you to open it instead of me. But what about vehicle doors? Do cowboys always open them for ladies?"

"Mostly they do. Sometimes it's just not convenient." She smiled. "Trying to get a bead on cowboy manners?"

"Aye."

"Opening doors is one part of it. Your hat's another part, like tipping it when you meet a woman. Or touching the brim with two fingers as you say goodbye."

"I've seen that in the movies." Wouldn't be hard to get in the habit of doing it. He followed her into Quinn's house where a table lamp was on in the living room and the scent of a wood fire lingered in the air.

"Talking about hats...when did you get yours?" She went left, flipped on an overhead and went into the kitchen.

"I stopped at a Western wear place after I picked up the car."

"I wondered if you'd found one in Scotland." She kept going. "The ice is this way."

"Didn't think of getting one in Scotland." Quinn kept a tidy kitchen. Not surprising. "Don't know if I could even get one, especially on short notice."

"But you must have been strongly motivated to own one before you arrived at the ranch." Opening the kitchen door, she turned on another light and walked out on an enclosed back porch.

"I figured it was the first step."

"For what?" She lifted the lid on a large freezer chest.

"Becomin' a cowboy."

She turned to him and smiled. "That's what you're going for?"

"Why not? I'm in Montana, livin' on a ranch, and looks like I'll have a top-notch riding teacher. You just gave me some tips on manners. What's left?"

"Well, there's something called the cowboy way." She started loading him up with bags of ice.

"Never heard of it. What's it mean?"

"I doubt I could explain it in a few words. In fact, I might not be the one to explain it at all. Quinn could do it way better. For example, did you happen to wonder why he had a rope handy to pull out that fawn?"

"I meant to ask him, but there was never time."

"He'd probably explain that as part of the cowboy way." She paused and counted the bags in his arms. "I think what you have plus what I can carry should be enough. If you'll take those out and put them in the trunk, I'll follow behind with a few more."

"All right."

"You don't have to wait for me. I'll be right behind you."

"I won't. I'm just takin' a minute to look at you. You're beautiful. Your glasses frame your face and emphasize your green eyes."

"They do?"

"Very well."

"Oh. Good, I guess. I do prefer them to the contacts."

"You're beautiful both ways. Now I need to get rid of this ice before my chest hair freezes." He retraced his way through the house, which wasn't as big as Kendra's but had similar cushy furniture and an appealing lived-in look.

A newspaper and a book lay in a basket near an easy chair and wildflowers in a Mason jar sat on the coffee table. The rural ambiance reminded him of Scotland. No wonder his gran and grandpa had spent several years in Montana. They'd been sheep farmers, and were sheep farmers, still.

He dumped the bags of ice into the trunk and added the ones Damaris brought out. Clutching bags of ice to his chest had cooled his entire body. He shouldn't have the same problem going back as he had coming here.

He put on a grand show as he helped her into the car, which made her laugh. Then he touched two fingers to the brim of his hat before closing the door and walking around to the driver's side.

Laying his hat on the dash, he climbed in. "How'm I doin'?"

"Spectacularly. You'll be a cowboy before you know it."

"Before you go back to California?" He started the car. This adventure had a time stamp. He'd be wise to remember that.

"I don't know. That's asking a lot of yourself."

"I usually do." He switched on the headlamps, turned the car around and started down the dirt road.

"Now, see, that's the sort of thing a cowboy would say. They give a hundred percent to whatever they take on."

"I don't know of any other way of bein'."

"Then you're more than halfway there. But you might need to pace yourself. By now you must be running on fumes."

"Aye. Lack of sleep is catchin' up with me. There's just one more thing I want to do when we get back. Then I'll head inside."

"What's that?"

"If the band's still playin', I want to dance with you once more."

"In the grass?"

"Up on the platform."

Her breath hitched.

"I know you can do it." He glanced over at her. "Are you willin'?"

"Yes. And if I make a fool of myself, so what?"

"That's the spirit, lass."

9

The band wasn't playing after Damaris and Rory unloaded the bags of ice and delivered them to the ranch kitchen. She paused to check out the situation before leaving the front porch. "Maybe we won't get that dance, after all." She was disappointed for his sake but relieved for herself.

"They haven't put away their instruments, so I don't think they're done for the night. Come on." He grabbed her hand and started down the steps. "Let's see if they know one of my favorite Scottish tunes. If they play it in the right tempo, it's perfect for dancin'."

She hurried with him over to the platform. Letting go of her hand, he vaulted onto it, not bothering to walk around to the steps. He might not have enjoyed working in the distillery warehouse, but he was built for heavy lifting.

The band members nodded as he talked with them. When he hopped down and came back to her, he was all smiles. "They know it! They'll play one last set before they leave. We made it in time."

"That's great!"

He cupped his big hands around her shoulders. "I hear the words comin' out of that beautiful mouth, but those green eyes say somethin' different. Am I askin' too much?"

"No. I want to. Mostly."

He met her gaze and smiled. "Then let's dance."

"What's the tune?"

"*Comin' Thro' the Rye.*"

"Oh! I love that one, too."

"Did you know it's a poem by Robbie Burns?"

"No, that's news to me."

"It's also about—hey, they're startin' already. Let's go." He led her quickly around to the steps.

She didn't have time to think as she dashed up to the platform and he swept her into his arms. His firm grip kept her steady and the music, a song from the *Outlander* soundtrack, gladdened her heart.

The band didn't happen to have a bagpipe, but they had a fiddle. She'd spent hours absorbed in the soundtrack and could fill in the sexy groan of a bagpipe, no problem.

Soon after she and Rory took the floor, Zane and Mandy joined them. Mandy called out a cheerful *You go, Damaris!* That should have thrown her off her game, but by some miracle she didn't trip over Rory's feet.

Bryce and Nicole took the floor next. As they danced closer, Nicole caught Damaris' attention and gave her a thumbs-up. That didn't make her stumble, either. Amazing. She wouldn't question it. She'd just enjoy.

Gradually the platform filled with McGavins and then Sawyers. Conditions were crowded, but Rory navigated the territory with deft twists and turns. She didn't trip or stumble. Not once.

When the tune ended, Rory spun her under his arm one last time before pulling her in for a quick hug. "Brilliant," he murmured in her ear before letting her go.

Mandy came over with Zane. "Hey, girlfriend. Am I wrong, or did you used to hate dancing?"

"I did, but Rory gave me some tips. It's just patterns, really. And it's more fun than I thought." She was short of breath but thrilled that she'd made it through without screwing up.

"Well done, Rory." Mandy gave him an approving glance.

Zane smiled. "It's in the genes, cuz. If you're a McGavin, you dance. End of story."

"Or a Sawyer." Brendan came over with Jo. "I'm glad to see you've recovered from that little swim you took earlier, son."

"I have. Good thing you were there to administer CPR on the fawn." He smiled at Jo. "And thanks for wadin' in to help pull me out. I hope your boots are all right."

"They'll be fine. It was like old times. I've been soaked by that creek more times than I can count. Kendra and I—" She paused as the music began. "I guess we should either leave the floor or dance."

"I'll choose to leave," Rory said. "Dancin' to that tune was special, but now I'm done for the night." He glanced at Damaris. "You probably want to stay, though. Thanks for—"

"I'll walk you to the house."

"That would be nice." He waited for her to go ahead of him down the steps.

She glanced over her shoulder at Mandy and Zane. "Are you guys taking off soon?"

"We're gonna dance for a little while," Zane said.

"Good. I'll be back." She went quickly down the steps.

"No rush," Mandy called after her. "That last dance woke me up, so I'm good for another half-hour or so."

"Thanks for walking with me," Rory said.

She smiled. "It's the friendly thing to do."

"And I feel like we're friends."

"I feel like that, too. As if we've known each other longer than ten hours."

"Is that what it's been?"

"Give or take." She pulled her phone out of her pocket. "To be exact, it's been nine hours and forty-three minutes."

"Are you saying you noted my arrival time?"

"I did. It's not every day a ginger Scotsman comes into my life."

"Hm."

"What?"

"Now that you mention our first meeting, I remember you saying I look like that Jamie Fraser character from *Outlander*."

"Well, you do. That's not a bad thing. And by the way, *Comin' Thro' the Rye* is on the soundtrack for the TV series."

"I didn't know that."

"It was a great choice."

"Because it reminded you of Jamie?"

"A little bit."

He paused at the base of the steps and flashed her a teasing smile. "Are you telling me you only fancy me because I remind you of that bloke?"

"Oh, absolutely." She maintained a deadpan stare. "It has nothing to do with your gallant behavior, your willingness to risk your life for an innocent fawn, or your ability to laugh at yourself. Or your amazing dancing ability."

He laughed. "Good. Just so we're clear." His gaze met hers. "I didn't finish tellin' you what that song is about."

"No, but I always thought it described two sweethearts meeting."

"It's a wee bit more specific than that, at least that's what I've been told."

"Oh?"

He drew her closer. "It's about makin' love."

"Is that so?"

"Aye." He combed his fingers through her hair. "I should be goin' inside."

The warmth in his eyes played havoc with her breathing. "Yes, you should."

"Can't seem to make myself leave."

"If you don't get some sleep, you'll be too tired for anything tomorrow."

"Not for some things."

Heat blasted through her. "I see."

"Like a riding lesson." He cupped her cheek. "Any secluded trails around here?"

"Uh-huh." She took a shaky breath. "But you need to be rested for that or you might fall off your horse."

"Good point, lass. Then I guess it's time to kiss you goodnight." Leaning down, he covered her mouth with his, lingered for a dizzying few seconds and released her. Touching two fingers to the brim of his hat, he turned and went up the steps, taking them two at a time.

She stood there, lips tingling and pulse racing. Once she could breathe again, she returned to the party just as Mandy and Zane arrived back at the head table.

Zane glanced at the table and picked up an empty water pitcher. "I'll go fill this and be back."

"Thanks, sweetie." Mandy leaned against the table and smiled at Damaris. "Having fun?"

"Big fun. We'll probably hang out a little while I'm here."

"I should hope so. You two are adorable together. I've never seen you dance like that."

"Because I never have."

"I only wish he didn't live so damn far away."

"Maybe that's a good thing. When I'm involved in my research, I don't have time to—"

"For a man like that, you'd make the time."

"Okay, you could be right. Fortunately, I don't have to figure that out. I'm on vacation this week. No work and all play."

"Then make the most of it, girlfriend."

"Don't worry. I plan to soak up every single minute."

<u>10</u>

Where in the bloody hell was he? Rory sat straight up in a bed that was not his own, a narrow mattress that fit one person, barely, in his case. Reaching up, he touched wooden slats. A second bed was above his.

Right. He was in the bottom bunk in a bedroom that used to belong to a couple of his American cousins. He was in *Montana.*

He'd left his phone on the floor beside the bed. Leaning over to pick it up, he checked the time. A little after five in the morning. Pitch black outside his window.

But people were up. Noises came from somewhere in the house. He took a deep sniff of coffee brewing. Was Damaris awake yet?

The combination of hot coffee and the prospect of seeing her propelled him out of bed. Pulling on his jeans, he crossed the hall to the bathroom and glanced at her door. Closed. A light was on down the hall in the master bedroom, and another light at the other end, in the living room.

The ranch was coming to life, a bit like his gran and grandpa's sheep farm did every morning about this time. He hadn't stayed overnight with them since he was a kid but he used to love being there. He'd forgotten how much.

He washed up quickly without taking time to shave. Whatever was happening on this ranch first thing in the morning, he wanted in on it. He could come back and shave later, before he drove into town. No reason to go now. Nothing would be open.

Dressing quickly, he put on his work boots and a long-sleeved t-shirt. Then he finger-combed his hair, grabbed his hat off the dresser and headed for the kitchen.

Aunt Kendra's words filtered out to him. "I'm proud of her, holding off until this morning. Although Wes might have hoped she'd wait until tomorrow."

"He's okay." Quinn's voice. "He's used to losing sleep. Part of the job."

"I'm gonna head down there." An unfamiliar voice. Then the man who'd driven the buckboard came through the kitchen door. He paused. "Hey, Rory."

"Good mornin'." He scrambled for a name. "Jim, right?"

"That's right." The lanky cowboy offered his hand. "Jim Underwood, Faith's dad."

"Is Rory up?" Kendra came to the doorway. "Wow, I thought for sure you'd sleep in."

"I'm not much for that."

She smiled. "Because you're a McGavin. Want coffee?"

"Yes, please."

"I'll get him some," Quinn called from the kitchen. "You're going to be so glad you woke up early, son."

"Why?"

"I'll let Kendra tell you."

Her blue eyes sparkled. "A mare is in labor."

"No kiddin'?"

"Yep. She's one of the few mares we board. Last year her family decided to breed her and we've been on pins and needles because she might have delivered yesterday. Luckily she waited."

"I'm gonna go check on the situation," Jim said. "See how Wes is doing. I'll text you if we're getting close."

"Do that," Kendra said. "Rory, if you're hungry, there's toast and jam. We've both had that because we don't want to start breakfast yet. She could give birth any time, now."

He walked into the kitchen. "Toast is fine. I can make it. Is Wes a vet?"

"He sure is." Quinn handed him a steaming mug of coffee. "Evidently you've been paying attention."

"I can't take the credit." He carried the mug over to the counter and popped some bread into the toaster. "Damaris let me study her spreadsheet of family connections."

Kendra laughed. "I love it! That sounds just like Damaris."

"What sounds just like me?"

Rory turned around as Damaris walked barefoot into the kitchen wearing her dressing gown covered with equations. Her cheeks bloomed with the soft pink of someone who'd just climbed out of bed. She hadn't bothered to comb her hair and it framed her face in a glorious, shining tangle.

Bloody sexy. Rory battled the urge to go over there, gather her close and kiss those rosy lips.

She glanced at him and blinked. "Rory?" She pulled her glasses out of her dressing gown pocket and put them on. "What are you doing up this early?"

"Couldn't sleep. How about you?"

"I heard people out here talking and smelled coffee, but I could swear the last few mornings things started later than this."

"They did," Kendra said. "Jim got us up. He spent the night in the barn with Licorice. She's in labor."

"She *is*? That's fabulous! I can't believe I forgot that she was ready to foal any day. You told me and then I got wrapped up in the wedding yesterday and totally spaced it."

"Jim was on the job," Quinn said. "He made several visits to the barn during the party and kept us informed. Then he decided to sleep there."

"Is Wes here? Can we go down there? How soon do you think—"

"It'll be soon, judging from what Wes has texted us," Quinn said. "Jim just left to eyeball the progress for himself. And yes, you can go down with us. We'll be leaving soon."

"I need to get dressed, then." She started out of the kitchen.

"Hang on a sec," Kendra said. "Do you want me to fix you a to-go mug of coffee?"

"That would be great. I'll be right back."

"How about toast and jam?" Rory called after her.

"That'd be great, too!"

He toasted more bread and made jam sandwiches they could eat on the way to the barn. "I've never seen a foal born. Lambs, but never a foal."

"Lambs." Kendra leaned against the counter and gazed at him as she drank her coffee. "That brings back memories. Do your grandparents still have a sheep farm?"

"Aye, they do." He finished up the sandwiches.

"You can put them in these." She handed him a box of sandwich bags. "I remember the sheep farm they had while they lived here. They tried so hard to make a go of it, but we have more predators in Montana than they were used to. They got pretty discouraged."

"They told me that. They liked Montana and the folks they met, but it's easier for them to raise sheep there."

"No doubt. I'm so glad you decided to come for a visit. It's been less than twenty-four hours and you already feel like part of the family."

He chuckled. "Maybe because I got myself in trouble right away."

"I have to admit that creek episode reminded me of things my boys used to do. Still do, on occasion."

"Same here." Quinn polished off his coffee and put his mug in the dishwasher. "Very familiar."

"So why did you have a rope with you yesterday?" Ever since Damaris had brought that up, it had been niggling at him.

"Habit. A couple of times I didn't have a rope when I wished I'd had one. Eventually I made it a practice to always carry one tied to my saddle." He glanced at Kendra. "Even when I'm going to a wedding."

"Yeah, yeah, I'll admit I was wrong to poke fun at you for that." Kendra took a to-go mug out of the cupboard and filled it for Damaris. "After yesterday's deal, I'll carry one, too. If I'd had one, I could have thrown it to Rory."

"That's right," Quinn said. "Brendan said the same thing. He doesn't always carry one, either. Glad I made a couple of converts. The more ropes, the better."

"I'd be a convert, too," Rory said. "Except I don't know how to throw one so taking it would make no sense."

"I can teach you." Damaris walked in wearing jeans, boots and a long-sleeved t-shirt like his, only hers was moss green instead of black. She'd pulled her hair into a ponytail.

"You know how to rope?"

"Kendra taught me." She took the to-go mug Kendra handed her. "Thanks."

"And to think I taught you to rope without knowing the physics of how to build a perfect flat loop. Thanks to you, I do, now."

"I don't know the physics of it," Quinn said. "Guess I have more to learn about roping, after all."

Damaris shrugged. "Not really, if you've been doing it all your life. I was just amusing myself, seeing if I could reduce it to an equation." She glanced around. "Are we ready to go?"

"I think so," Kendra said. "Rory made your toast and jam into sandwiches so you could take it with you."

"Yum. Thanks." She smiled at him. "I'm so excited about this. I only remember one other time you had a foal born here. It was on a school night and my parents wouldn't let me stay."

"I'd forgotten you missed that one." Kendra picked up her phone. "Before we leave, let me text Jim and see if we need to bring coffee or food for Wes." She tapped on her screen and waited for an answer. "Wes is okay. Ingrid came about an hour ago and brought him stuff."

"Wes's sweetheart is one of the baker ladies?" Rory glanced over at Damaris and got a subtle thumbs-up.

"She is." Quinn laughed. "Damaris, I wish I'd had you around to make me a spreadsheet when I first came to town."

"I keep telling Kendra I'm only an email or text away."

"I'll keep that in mind. Okay, let's move out." Quinn started toward the front door. "There's a chill in the air. Anybody need a jacket?"

"I'm from Scotland. I'm used to it."

"I'm too excited to be cold," Damaris said. "Go ahead. We'll follow you guys."

Rory waited for her to go out. Then he stepped into the brisk morning and pulled the door closed. "We're off." He hurried down the steps and handed her a sandwich bag.

"Thanks for making these. Can you hold my coffee for a minute?"

"Sure."

She took the sandwich out and stuffed the bag in her jeans pocket. "I can take my coffee, now." She sipped from the hole in the lid. "Mm. Best breakfast ever."

"Company's good, too."

"Yeah. I'm so glad I woke up."

"Me, too." He bit into his sandwich.

"I don't think Kendra realized how much I wanted to see this or she would have come in to get me. I guess you wouldn't have knocked on my door, either."

"Would you have liked me to?"

"Absolutely! Who wants to sleep when something like this is happening?" She took another bite.

"Some people would. For all I knew, you stayed up partyin' with your friends and needed the rest."

"I didn't stay much later, but even if I had, I wouldn't care whether I got enough sleep or not. I'd want to be here. Wouldn't you?"

"Aye. You know, it's amazin', though, how I just happened to come over to America when my cousin was gettin' married. And this mornin' a foal is bein' born, and it's not like that happens every day on this ranch, either."

"It doesn't. Kendra runs a riding and boarding stable, not a breeding operation. The mare that gave birth when I was a kid was a similar deal. The mare was boarded here and her family thought it would be cool to breed her."

"Is that mare still here?"

"No. Not her foal, either. I played with that filly a lot, but then about a year after that, the family moved out of state and took the mare and her filly with them."

"Kendra didn't say whether this mare's family is here. Didn't sound like they are or they'd be down at the barn right now."

"They're out of the country. Kendra said the teenager who rides Licorice was heartbroken to miss this, but her dad unexpectedly got some important job overseas and the family will be gone for a year. They're paying Kendra to raise the foal for them."

"Tough break for that girl."

"Yep. I like to think that in her shoes I would have figured out how to stay in Montana, maybe with a friend's family. But then again, I would miss my folks, especially if they were that far away."

"I'm attached to mine, too."

"Family's important." She was walking fast now, eager to witness the birth of the foal.

He was eager, too. Especially because he'd be sharing it with her.

11

Until this morning, Damaris had focused all her energy on April's big day. And on Rory, once he'd arrived on the scene. Even though she'd been told about Licorice's potential due date, the news had been buried in the cheerful chaos of wedding preparations.

The closest she'd been to the barn since her arrival had been yesterday when she'd climbed aboard Fifty Shades. She'd fallen in love with this vintage hip-roofed structure as a child and loved it still. Stepping through the wide double doors brought a rush of pleasure. Rory helped her pull the sliding door shut behind them.

The barn looked the same and smelled the same—a distinctive blend of fresh hay, seasoned wood, oiled leather and horse sweat. Aisle lights created a soft ambiance she'd always cherished. Early morning was her favorite time here. Kendra and her boys had kept it exactly as it had been for years, a peaceful environment for people and animals to commune.

Some of the horses were unfamiliar and others were old friends. Licorice's stall had to be in the middle since that's where Quinn, Kendra and Jim stood talking.

On the way there she introduced Rory to Jake, the gelding with Tennessee Walker lineage who'd been added when she was in high school. Then she had him meet Strawberry, a reliable saddle horse for beginners. Someone else must have claimed Strawberry yesterday or Quinn would have put Rory on him.

Winston, the butterscotch and white paint Kendra had ridden for the wedding, was at the far end of the barn, his head over the stall door, checking out the proceedings. He'd been the kingpin for years and usually he was talkative. But he was quiet this morning, as if he knew a mellow mood would comfort the mare through her labor.

Eeyore, the old gray horse Mandy and Jo shared, poked his head out of the stall across the aisle from Winston. How Damaris had yearned for a horse of her own, especially after Mandy got Eeyore. But a horse wasn't practical for a girl destined for advanced degrees, likely from universities on the West or East Coast. Her parents had been right about that.

When she and Rory reached Licorice's stall, she walked over and peeked in. The mare was lying on a clean bed of straw, her head toward the back wall. Wes was crouched beside her, running a hand over her swollen belly.

"Makes sense that she'd be black with a name like Licorice," Rory murmured as he came up beside her.

"She's not only black, she has a white star on her forehead like Black Beauty. You can't see it from this angle, though."

"Who's Black Beauty?"

"You don't know that story?"

"Can't say I do."

"It's a cherished classic for young horse lovers, especially girls. I read it."

"So did I." Kendra came over to join them. "I'm sure Kathryn talked her folks into getting Licorice for her because she loved that book. She wanted her own Black Beauty, although the one in the story was a gelding, not a mare."

Jim snorted. "This hasn't exactly been a storybook horse."

"No, but she's a lot better than she was," Kendra said.

"Thanks to you and your patience." Quinn walked over with Jim.

"That's the God's truth," Jim said. "Not sure I would have been that patient with a horse who threw me and put me in a wheelchair."

Rory frowned. "She did?"

"Broke Kendra's leg," Quinn said. "It wasn't the horse's fault that she'd learned bad habits. Still, I'm glad I wasn't here to see that."

"If I'd given up on her, no telling what her future would have been like."

Quinn's expression softened. "Not good. You did the right thing. I just don't like thinking of you being hurt."

"Neither did the boys, but it was my call and I don't regret keeping her and continuing to train her. She's calmer, now. She even tolerates men."

"Tolerate is the right word," Quinn said. "She never has warmed up to me."

Jim made a face. "She doesn't much care for me, either."

Kendra smiled. "Yet you spent the night to be sure she wouldn't go into labor all alone."

"Didn't want her to be scared. It's her first time. But this whole operation would've been a lot easier in the birthing stall we fixed for her in the other barn, the one she flatly refused to enter. She might be a more reliable saddle horse these days, but I wager she'll always be stubborn."

Quinn glanced at Kendra and chuckled. "I'm beginning to understand why you've bonded with this animal."

She smiled and batted her eyelashes. "Is that so?"

"Uh-huh." He put an arm around her shoulders. "But then, I've always loved a challenge."

"So have I." She gave him a quick kiss. "I'm going in to see my girl." She opened the stall door and stepped inside. "Hey, Wes." She hunkered down next to the mare. "What do you think?"

"She's coming along fine. If you want to watch her for a bit, I'll go stretch my legs."

"By all means."

He came out of the stall, stripped off his surgical gloves and shook hands with Rory. "Glad you made it over to visit. Didn't get a chance to talk with you yesterday, but I heard you just accidentally showed up on Ryker's big day. Great timing."

Rory smiled. "Dumb luck."

Whatever he chose to call it, Damaris was grateful. He might have visited his cousins at some point in the future, but chances were slim-to-none she would have been staying at Wild Creek Ranch.

Wes stood well over six feet, but he had to lift his head slightly to meet Rory's gaze. "You probably haven't had time to look around Eagles Nest, but it has a lot to recommend it."

"I thought so when I drove through yesterday. Almost stopped at Pie in the Sky."

Wes beamed. "You gotta go there. I'm prejudiced, but I've never eaten better pastries. The coffee's good, too."

"If that weddin' cake is an example, I'm a fan."

"Wasn't it terrific? Ingrid baked that one. Wedding cakes are her specialty. She made that custom cake topper, too."

"I meant to ask about that. I've never seen one like it."

"The peace symbol was for April and the Air Force logo was for Ryker."

"I get the Air Force part, but why the peace symbol for April?"

"She's a pacifist," Damaris said.

"And she married Ryker? Wasn't he in the military for years?"

"Sure was. He's a soldier to the bone. That's why they broke up after graduation. But they love each other and they're making it work."

"That impresses me. You could tell durin' the ceremony how much they care about each other. Knowin' this makes it even more special. I'm glad I was here."

"Wes," Kendra called out. "Her water just broke."

"Show time." Wes ducked back in with Kendra. "If you'll hold her head and talk to her, I'll handle the business end."

Damaris and Rory stood to the right of the stall door. Quinn and Jim took the other side.

"Holler if you need anything, son," Quinn said.

"I will, Dad. This one looks like it'll be textbook."

"That's what we like to hear."

Rory stood close enough that his shoulder touched Damaris. "That's something, April and Ryker working through their differences."

She nodded, savoring the proximity. "They overcame the odds."

"I guess you do when it's important enough." He lowered his voice. "I've been wantin' to kiss you since you walked into the kitchen."

Nice to know she wasn't the only one having those thoughts. "Were you, now?"

"You're smilin'. Were you thinkin' about that, too?"

"Maybe."

He slipped his fingers through hers. "Is this all right?"

She squeezed his hand. "Perfect." She took a shaky breath. An exciting event and an exciting man by her side. Potent stuff. "It's starting."

His breathing was unsteady, too. His grip tightened as the mare groaned and a translucent white membrane appeared beneath her wrapped tail. "This is very cool."

"Uh-huh."

"I used to love watching lambs come into the world."

"Where?" She kept her attention on the mare.

"My gran and grandpa's farm."

"Used to?"

"Haven't gone out for lambin' season in years."

"Why not?"

"Busy with school, then the job. Couldn't justify it. It's not like I'll be raisin' sheep."

"It's not like I'll be raising horses, either, but this is...oh! I see a hoof inside that membrane!"

"And there's another hoof. And its little nose!"

"Here comes its whole head...come on, little baby, come on...push, Licorice." Her heartbeat picked up. "Push, girl."

"She's doing great," Wes said. "We're halfway there."

"She is doing great," Kendra crooned. "What a good momma you are, Licorice. What a good momma."

"Come on, little guy." Rory's voice was gruff with emotion. "You can do it."

Wes chuckled. "Could be a girl, too, Rory."

"I just have a feelin' it's a boy."

Damaris squeezed his hand. "Maybe you're psychic."

"No, I—we'll find out in a few minutes."

"Looks like he didn't take after his momma," Quinn said as Wes wiped the membrane clinging to the foal's nose.

"See?" Rory sounded pleased. "Quinn thinks it's a boy."

"I do, Rory," Quinn said. "Just like you, I have a hunch."

"I can't see from here," Kendra said. "What color? Black?"

"No," Jim said. "Looks like he'll be a bay like his daddy."

"That works," Kendra said. "His daddy's a handsome stallion. Now you've got me convinced this foal's a boy."

"We'll know soon," Wes said. "Almost there...and we're done." He gently pushed aside the membrane. "Congratulations, Licorice. You have a son."

Rory grinned. "Knew it."

"He has a very interesting white marking on his forehead," Damaris said. "Like a crescent moon."

"To me it looks like an eclipse," Rory said. "Could be of the moon or the sun."

"I like that idea," Kendra said. "Wasn't Eclipse that famous racehorse from the seventeen hundreds?"

"That's why it sounds so familiar!" Damaris glanced up at Rory. "He was a famous British racehorse. Did you ever hear of him?"

"I don't know much about racing."

"I'm no expert, but I think his bloodline continued down to a bunch of Kentucky Derby winners." She glanced over at Kendra. "Does that ring a bell?"

"It does. I think even Secretariat. Quinn? What do you know about Eclipse?"

"I've read about him, now that you mention it. The horse with the big heart, literally. But are we allowed to name him? He's not ours."

"He isn't, but Kathryn gave me naming privileges. She wants this foal to have a name from the get-go so he will get used to hearing it from day one."

"Then I'd go with Eclipse. What do you think, Jim?"

"Can't do better than an unbeaten champion with a big heart."

"I agree," Kendra said. "Rory, it looks like you've named this foal. Aren't you glad you took a notion to come to America? Your timing was perfect."

"Aye, it was."

<u>**12**</u>

"I need to talk to you, lass." Rory had searched for a moment to speak to Damaris privately and had finally found one as they helped clear the dining table after a hearty breakfast. "It doesn't feel right not tellin' Kendra the reason why I showed up now, but sayin' somethin' when she's excited about the foal seems wrong. Any advice?"

"I'd wait a little longer. Like you said, this is a special time for her. Maybe tonight over dinner would be better."

"I'll do that, then."

"I know you're not looking forward to explaining yourself, but I wouldn't worry about her reaction when you finally do tell her. She's so happy that you're here that she'll take whatever you say in stride."

"I hope so. On a different subject, I thought I'd shower and drive into town. Would you like to—"

"Show you around Eagles Nest? I'd love to. But let me jump in the shower ahead of you. I need to wash my hair so I'll take longer to get ready than you will."

"Fair enough. Go ahead, then. I'll help in the kitchen until the bathroom's free."

"Okay."

He watched her walk away, enjoying the easy sway of her curvy hips. His tadger reacted in a predictable fashion. This affair she'd proposed was on the back burner until after the shopping trip. Then they required some private time.

She'd mentioned possibly taking a horseback ride later today. Had she arranged for that? Should he? He'd never navigated a situation like this before.

Carrying a stack of plates into the kitchen where Kendra and Quinn were working together, he set the plates next to the sink. "Damaris and I are planning to drive into town once we both get cleaned up, if that's all right."

"Certainly. Good idea." Kendra glanced up from the pan she was scouring. "Quinn and I were seriously thinking of taking a nap."

"A nap?"

Quinn loaded the plates in the dishwasher. "Maybe you'd call it a lie-down. We're bushed."

"I can understand. A weddin' and a foalin' would take it out of a person."

"Not to mention a lack of sleep," Kendra said. "And lack of cuddle time."

"Right." He admired them for being open about their delight in each other. "And the foal's probably fine for a little while." Was that true? Must be or they wouldn't take a nap.

"Cody will keep an eye on those two for the rest of the day." Kendra rinsed the pan. "Zane said he'll come over, too. We sent Jim home for the day. We didn't book any trail rides this weekend, so we have plenty of folks available to monitor our new arrival."

"That's when you schedule trail rides? On the weekend?"

She nodded. "Trail rides on the weekend and lessons during the week. I cancelled all my lessons for last week. Faith went ahead with hers but I just didn't have the time. I'll start back tomorrow."

"That reminds me. Damaris mentioned possibly takin' a horseback ride later."

"That's fine. I'll let Cody and Zane know. Just walk down to the barn and one of them will fix you up." She gazed at him. "But please don't jump in the creek today. Damaris could probably save you, but I'd rather not test it."

He smiled. "I'll stay out of the creek."

"Excellent." She gave him a hug. "Go take your shower. We've got this."

He sensed that she and Quinn wanted alone time, so he left the kitchen. But when he walked down the hall, the shower was still running in the bathroom he shared with Damaris.

How sweet it would be if he could walk in there, strip off his clothes and get into the shower with her. But they hadn't reached that stage and besides, he was in someone else's home. A move like that would be in bad taste.

Instead he went into his own room and texted his brother. It was early Sunday evening in Scotland. Might be a good time to reach Aleck and check in. All he'd managed yesterday was a quick text before he'd walked up onto the ranch house porch and surprised the hell out of Aunt Kendra.

Aleck didn't return the text. He called. "I was plannin' to ring you in about an hour. You beat me to it."

"Well, here I am. What's goin' on?"

"Sure enough, that boss of yours contacted ma and da."

"No!"

"Oh, yeah. Ravin' about breach of promise, which is insane because you never offered marriage to her."

"I swear I did not."

"She's claimin' that you did. That you proposed, took her virginity and then reneged on the deal. It's a worst-case scenario, one of those *he said, she said* issues. Naturally her father believes everythin' his precious daughter says."

"What now?"

"Unfortunately, when you left the country, it looked like an admission of guilt."

"Bloody hell. I was only tryin' to—"

"Be a gentleman about it. I know. You said as much when you were standin' in my office. You may be a gentleman, Rory, but you're not dealin' with a lady. Or a gentleman. Her father is no better than she is."

His stomach bottomed out. He'd worked so hard for this. Could one misstep ruin everything? "What do you think I should do?"

"Come home and defend yourself. The sooner you can get a flight, the better."

He wanted to go back and tackle this problem. He did. But...Damaris. "I was plannin' to book the return flight far enough out that it wouldn't be as bloody expensive as the one that got me here."

"To hell with the money. I'm good for it and I know you'll pay me back. This is your future we're talkin' about. I'll represent you. We'll get this taken care of and ensure that her father doesn't ruin your good name in the distillery business. That career is your dream, and I won't stand by and let him derail it."

"You're a good brother." He took a deep breath. "This is a lot to take in."

"It is. But there's only one way to deal with a bully, and we have two of them, Catriona and her father. Together we'll confront them and back them down."

"The thing is, I—"

"Since she mounted a campaign to get you into her bed, I need to document everything you remember about her seductive behavior toward you. Then tell me exactly how she threatened you afterward. I guarantee we'll win this thing."

"I don't understand. Is her da tryin' to force me into marryin' her?"

"Yes, but we'll—"

"Why would he do such a thing? Forcin' two people into marriage won't make them love each other. More likely they'll hate each other."

"Here's the way they presented it to ma and da. You're attracted to her or you wouldn't have had sex with her. Sure, you got cold feet after the fact, but many prospective bridegrooms get wet feet. Once you're bound in holy matrimony—"

"Unholy is more like it."

"Regardless, she and her father believe that your passion for her will save the day and you'll realize, as men ultimately do, that great sex, not to mention a lucrative job with her da's company, is worth givin' up your freedom for."

"Sex with her was nice, but it wasn't *that* great and besides, it's not just about sex and certainly not about career advancement, much as I'm focused on that. Yesterday I attended a weddin' of two people who are so in love it sticks out all over them. I'm not settlin' for less."

"I'm not askin' you to settle for anythin'. I'm askin' you to come home and take care of this guddle. Catriona and her da need a smack-down and I'm ready to give it to them."

"I appreciate that loyalty and support. Believe me, I do."

"There's a *but* comin'. I can feel it."

"I rather not come home just yet."

"Why not?"

"I just got here yesterday, in the middle of Ryker McGavin's weddin'. I've met the whole family and the extended family. They've been friendly and welcomin'. This mornin' I was there when a foal was born. I got to name it."

"You're havin' a good time. That's wonderful. But the longer you stay over there, the more time they'll have to smear your reputation. If you come home now, you'll have a good chance of salvagin' it and gettin' hired by another distillery. The longer you wait, the dimmer your hopes for doin' that."

"I'm just gettin' to know the folks here." And one particular person who had turned off the shower and at this moment was drying off her curvy body…

"Rory McGavin, I recognize that tone of voice. Is there a woman in the picture?"

He thought how to answer.

"Never mind. Your silence speaks volumes."

"She'll only be here a week. Then she's goin' back to California. She works bloody hard and this is her first vacation in four years."

"And she wants to spend it with you."

"Aye, she does. I understand this is dire. I do. But would it matter so much whether I come back now or in a few days?"

Aleck groaned. "Like I said, the longer you stay over there, the worse you'll look and the harder it will be to give these schemin' bastards the drubbin' they deserve."

"I'm grateful for your support, Aleck. It means the world to me. I could use a bit of time to think this through."

"Right. I know what you need a bit of time for."

"Are you in court in the mornin'?"

"Not tomorrow. I'll be in the office until noon."

"I'll call you at quarter-to-eleven."

"You do realize that's quarter-to-five your time."

"Aye. These are ranch folks. They get up early, like gran and grandpa. Bein' here reminds me of stayin' out at the farm. Do you remember that?"

"Vividly. It taught me that I'm not cut out to be a sheep farmer. Those memories got me through law school."

"I kind of liked it. Watchin' that foalin' was somethin'. Anyway, I'll call you in the mornin'."

"Keep your wits about you, Rory."

"I will." He disconnected.

Bloody hell. If only he'd kept his tadger in his pants. Except then he wouldn't have been motivated to make this trip and he didn't regret that one bit. Bein' here felt right. Leavin' tomorrow, which was what Aleck wanted him to do, felt wrong.

13

Damaris offered to drive the rental car into town, but Rory was determined to master driving on what he called the wrong side of the road.

"I do sympathize." She controlled the urge to wince when he swerved dangerously close to a ditch. "I rented a car when I was in Scotland on a self-driving tour."

"You were in Scotland? When?"

"After I finished graduate school."

"Where did you go?"

"Inverness, mostly."

"What a coincidence. Right in my back yard. What made you pick that area?"

"Drumossie Moor, where the Battle of Culloden was fought. And…just the Highlands in general."

"Ah, now I get the picture. You were lookin' for the ghost of Jamie Fraser."

"In a way. It was an *Outlander* tour."

"Did you find him, then?"

"No. But I loved taking that tour. Except for driving on the wrong side of the road. That was scary as hell."

"But it's not the wrong side of the road. *This* is." He glanced at her and smiled.

She smiled back. "It's hard to believe you never watched the series. They filmed so much around your home stomping grounds."

"I was nose-to-the-grindstone finishin' up my degree, takin' odd jobs to pay the tuition. Heard somethin' about it, paid no attention."

"I know how that is when you're into a subject. You must be as excited about making whiskey as I am about solving the mysteries of black holes."

"It fascinates me. When you decide to make Scotch for a livin' you know you'll be addin' to the legacy of all those who've come before you." He eased off on the gas as they neared the edge of town. "Where should we start? The pub?"

"That would be appropriate, wouldn't it? But let's save it for last. I'm still full from breakfast."

"So am I. What, then?"

"Pills and Pop. They're open, now, but they have shorter hours on Sunday so we need to get that accomplished first."

"Makes sense."

"You'll need to pull in diagonally."

"I see how folks are doin' it." He maneuvered the little car into a spot in front of the vintage drugstore.

She made it out of the car before he did. Levering himself out of the tiny seat took effort. He plucked his hat from the dash and closed the door before joining her on the sidewalk.

When he put on his hat and tugged on the brim, he could have passed for a Montana boy. He stuck his thumbs in his belt loops and glanced up and down the street, a typical cowboy stance. "Not many folks walkin' around today."

No Montana cowboy sounded like that. "Most businesses are closed on Sunday."

"Pie in the Sky, too?"

"I'm afraid so, if you were counting on a treat there. Even though we can't go in most places, I thought we could stroll along Main Street so you can get the lay of the land. We can come back tomorrow when everything's open, including the bakery."

He frowned. "Aye. Unless..." He stared off into the distance and sighed.

"Do you have plans for tomorrow?"

"I'm not sure." Something was clearly bothering him. The sparkle had disappeared from his eyes.

"What's going on?"

"I'll tell you about it over a pint at the Guzzlin' Grizzly."

"All right." She hesitated. He'd suggested stopping there first. Maybe there was a reason. "Do you want to skip Pills and Pop and go back to the GG?"

He met her gaze. "Only if you've changed your mind."

"I haven't changed my mind, but maybe you've had second thoughts."

"Oh, I've had second thoughts." His smile returned. "Third, fourth and fifth thoughts. The more thoughts I have, the hotter I get."

"Okay, then." The look he was giving her sent a signal directly to her lady parts. "We'd better make our purchase."

"My purchase." He took her hand and started toward the Pills and Pop entrance.

"Does that mean I'm supposed to wander the aisles and pretend I don't know what you're buying?"

"That's how I'm picturin' it. I've never gone condom shoppin' with a woman. Seems like it would take the romance right out of it."

The romance? She chose not to bring attention to his use of the word, but it was telling that he had. Wild horses wouldn't drag that word out of her. But it was the only one that described this week's activity. She'd never had an affair and wouldn't know how to conduct one.

But a romance was in her wheelhouse. This encounter with Rory had all the trappings— two people from different parts of the world thrown together for a magical interlude. When their separate worlds pulled them apart, they'd be grateful to have shared one brief shining moment...

"Lass?"

She blinked.

Rory stood holding the glass front door of Pills and Pop while he waited for her to go inside.

"Whoops." She walked quickly through the doorway. "Took a little mental vacay."

"So you did." He came in and a bell tinkled as the door swung closed behind him. "You had a glazed look in your eyes and everythin'. Does that happen to you often?"

"Yes, I'm embarrassed to say. All the time at work. I start spinning a new theory in my head and it's like watching a movie. I'm in my own little bubble until something or someone pops me out of it."

"Were you thinkin' of work just now?"

"Um, no."

The corners of his mouth tilted up. He pitched his voice low. "Were you daydreamin' about me?"

"Maybe."

"I'll take that as a yes and be glad for it." He turned to inspect the fifties-styled combination diner and drugstore. "Looks like a movie set with those red booths and the black and white tile floor."

"They've had that décor ever since I can remember."

"Place isn't very busy this morning."

"It'll probably pick up around noon. People come in for lunch."

"Is that a workin' jukebox in the corner?"

"Yep. When I was in high school, we hung out here all the time—talking, eating, dancing."

"Dancin'? But I thought you—"

"April and Ryker danced. I was here for the talking and the food. The hot fudge sundaes are amazing."

"Now I wish I hadn't just finished breakfast."

"We can come back."

"Right." He sounded hesitant, though. "I'll go ahead and pick up what I came here for, if you'll point me in the right direction."

"Somewhere by the pharmacy window would be my guess."

"I'll be right back."

"And I'll wait here." If he considered it unromantic for her to tag along, she'd abide by his wishes. It was kind of cute that he felt that way.

"Do you have shoppin' to do?"

"Nope."

"Then I'll be quick."

"Take your time. I'll put some money in the jukebox."

He gave her a grin and a quick thumbs-up.

She was on her way to pick out a couple of tunes when Ellie Mae Stockton's voice floated up from the back of the store. "If it isn't my favorite Scotsman! Must be my lucky day!"

Oh, boy. Good luck navigating this one, Rory. She decided to hold off on playing the jukebox for a minute to see how he'd manage.

His deep voice carried to the front of the store. "It's good to see you, too, Ellie Mae."

"That *brogue*, Rory. Shades of Sean Connery. Not that you look anything like him, but if I close my eyes, I can imagine him standing right here. I worked on *Diamonds Are Forever*, you know."

"You worked in movies?"

"I did. You could, too. You have the face for it. And the build. Can I help you find something, dear boy?"

"No, thanks. I'm just—"

"I'm not sure what you're used to in Scotland, but I recommend this brand. They're very strong, but I'm told they feel like you're wearing nothing."

Rory's voice dropped to a murmur and Damaris choked back a laugh as she put money in the jukebox. Giggling under her breath, she chose Johnny Cash's *Ring of Fire*. That should aptly describe Rory's state of mind as Ellie Mae advised him on his condom purchase.

As *Ring of Fire* played on the glittering neon and chrome jukebox, she swayed to the music and considered what else to choose. She was still debating when an arm came around her waist. Her pulse skipped into high gear.

"I survived," Rory murmured. He kept his arm around her waist.

She gave him a sideways glance. "Congratulations."

"Made the whole thing go much faster. I just grabbed the first one she suggested and made a beeline for the cash register. What else are you goin' to play?"

"I can't decide."

"That one."

She laughed. "For the tune or the message behind it?"

"Both. You played *Ring of Fire*, knowin' I was sweatin' back there with Ellie Mae givin' me condom advice. Play this one for me."

"I guess that's fair." She punched the button for Lee Ann Womack's *I Hope You Dance.*

"And I hope you do. With me." He tugged her gently away from the jukebox.

"Now?"

"No one else is on the floor."

She glanced at his empty hands. "What did you do with the—"

"On the seat, first booth by the door."

She looked over. A small white bag sat on the red vinyl upholstery. This affair was happening. Eventually.

"The pattern's a three count. Waltz with me, Damaris." He didn't wait for an answer, just twirled her into his arms and began.

She stumbled.

"*One*-two-three, *one*-two-three." He began exaggerating his steps, dipping and turning with each count.

And she got it. Even better, her body got it. Waltzing was amazing. Who knew? "I love this!"

He grinned. "Patterns."

"Yeah! Patterns!" But that didn't explain why she was moving gracefully around the tiny dance floor. It didn't explain why her heart lifted each time the music of the chorus swelled around them. Or why she, who'd avoided dancing for years, didn't ever want this dance to end. The explanation was both simple and complicated.

Rory.

<u>**14**</u>

After leaving Pills and Pop, Rory walked with Damaris up one side of Main Street and down the other. He stopped to peer in store windows while she gave him a running commentary of her life here. Eventually he helped her back into the tiny rental, wedged himself in the driver's seat and headed for the Guzzling Grizzly.

"What do you think of my little town?"

"I like it. It reminds me of a Scottish village."

"Wow, I can't see that at all. For one thing, the architecture is completely different."

"Aye, that's a fact. And your primary road is straight as a tape measure while our village roads wind every which way. But the feel of it is the same as many small towns back home. I can tell from what you've said that folks know their neighbors and most have lived in Eagles Nest a long time."

"There's that. I moved to California years ago, but people still remember me. They ask about my parents. It's nice."

"It goes deeper than nice, I think. There's affection in your voice when you describe this place."

"I suppose there is. I have lots of good memories. I guess it'll always be home even though my parents have moved away."

"Ever thought of comin' back?"

"To stay?"

"Right. You clearly love it." He put on his turn signal and only had to wait for one car to pass before making a left into the Guzzling Grizzly parking lot.

"I do, but my work is in California. That said, this trip has taught me that I want to spend more time here than I have in the past. I don't want to lose my connection with the town or my friends."

"I've only been here one day and I don't want to lose my connection, either." He wasn't sure if he meant the town or her. Likely both.

"Good. Then we can stay in touch."

That sounded more casual than what he had in mind. "Good." He found a spot far from other vehicles, pulled in and cut the motor. But no matter how he tried to exit that wee car faster, he couldn't get around to her door before she was out and waiting for him.

She gestured to the glossy black pavement at her feet. "They did a fabulous job on this."

"Was it recently repaved?"

"Until a couple of weeks ago, it wasn't paved at all. The parking lot was dirt."

"Like in the Old West?"

"Exactly. Bryce and Michael had a big debate about whether paving it would destroy the rustic ambiance everyone loves. Michael wanted it paved and Bryce wanted to keep it the way it was."

"I see who won that argument."

"It wasn't so simple. Roxanne, Michael's wife, wanted to keep it dirt. Nicole, Bryce's fiancée, thought it should be paved. Kendra was the tie-breaker. She announced she was sick of getting her dancing boots muddy and it was high time the GG stepped into the twenty-first century. The debate was over."

"See, that's what I'm talkin' about. That's exactly how it would go in a Scottish village. With a question such as that, all manner of folks would stick an oar in. It would be a hot topic at the local pub."

"Well, this is our local pub." She led the way toward the front door. "And I understand it was a hot topic for days. Then Kendra weighed in and the matter was settled."

"She has that much influence?"

"It's subtle, but yes, she does. The McGavins are the most prominent family in town. With that name, you're not just connected to Eagles Nest, you're connected to its royalty."

He smiled. "Good to know." He grasped the polished brass handle on the front door. It's oval glass insert was etched with an image of a bear drinking a pint. "Is that the Guzzlin' Grizzly?"

"It is, now. Roxanne created that logo a year ago and it's been a smash hit. You can get t-shirts, mugs, sweatshirts—you name it. The GG

Country store will be on your right as you go in. Do you want to shop?"

"Not now, but I will before I leave town. I've already made the most important purchase of the day." Yet he might never use any. If he decided to leave tomorrow, he'd turned this alleged affair into a one-night stand.

Regardless of how his relationship with Catriona had turned out, he'd never been a fan of a one-and-done sexual experience. That smacked of racking up conquests and he loathed that mentality.

If he took a woman to bed, it was with the hope they'd enjoy many more encounters, maybe even discover a richer emotion than lust. He hated the idea of initiating something today and ending it tomorrow when he flew back to Scotland. He thought more of Damaris than that. He thought more of himself, for that matter.

Maybe she'd be fine with one night together, though. He wouldn't know until he asked. And he needed someone to talk to about the problems at home. Someone he trusted.

Business was light and a *Please Seat Yourself* sign was posted inside the door.

"Choose your spot," Damaris said. "We can sit anywhere since there's no live entertainment at the moment."

"Let's take that little table in front by the dance floor."

"No one will be performing until tonight."

"That's fine with me." He had information to impart and live music would only muck that up.

"Are you considering dancing to the canned music on the sound system? Because much as I enjoyed that waltz, I'd feel on display at the GG. It's a way bigger venue."

"I didn't plan to dance." *Note to self. Spontaneous dance invitations don't always work for Damaris Gataki.* "I just like sittin' where it's less claustrophobic."

"Okay, then. The two-top works fine."

"What should I do with my hat?"

"Up to you. The tendency in the GG is to keep it on. That's the safest place for it."

"Then I'll follow that custom." He pulled out her chair for her. Once she was tucked in, he took the opposite seat. "I was thinkin' a pint and some chips, but if you're hungrier than that, order away."

"That sounds like plenty, but do you mean potato chips or French fries?"

"I mean the kind that are cut up on the spot and tossed into hot oil. What do you call that?"

She smiled. "Fries. Over here, chips are thin slices of potato that are baked or fried, and usually they're mass-produced in factories and come in a sealed plastic bag."

"I got some of those in the airport in Chicago. I'd rather have the hot kind."

"Good man. So would I. Before we order, though, turn around and look at the art on the wall behind you. Quinn created that."

He swiveled in his chair, sucked in a breath and got up to walk closer. "Quinn did this?"

"Yes, and when it sells, he'll replace it with another. He has a studio behind his house and he spends nearly every morning there."

Rory pushed back his hat and gazed at a magnificent image of two mountain lions on a ledge, one reclining and one standing watch. It had to be at least six feet square. "What's this technique? I've never seen it before."

"It's called scratch board art. Quinn can explain it better than I can, but he covers the surface with black ink and then uses various tools to create what you see."

"Incredible." He walked over to the image and noticed a discreet price tag attached to a plaque. The work was called *Mated for Life.* It cost a small fortune.

He repositioned his hat. "And I thought he was Kendra's stable hand."

"As I said, he's a bit more than that."

"Clearly." He returned to the table. "Eagles Nest has depth."

"Yes, it does. It's taken me a while to realize it, myself."

"Admiring Quinn's work, I see." Jenny, one of the women from the table he'd occupied at the wedding, brought them glasses of water. She looked to be in her fifties, a down-to-earth lady who didn't worry about her hair turning gray.

He'd warmed to her immediately. "When I met Quinn yesterday," he said, "I had no idea there was this whole other side to him."

"He won't tell you, either. He's modest, our Quinn."

"Evidently."

"So! Welcome to the GG! I just have to say that sitting at your table last night was a highlight." She turned to Damaris. "Isn't this fellow a hoot and a half?"

"He is. I'm showing him around town today."

"Most everything's closed up, though."

"I know. I'm giving him an overview."

Jenny nodded. "Good idea. Then he knows which shops he wants to come back to. What are you two having?"

Rory gestured to Damaris. "You first."

"I'll have a frosted mug of that light ale you have on tap. And an order of fries."

"Perfect. Rory? How about you?"

"The same."

"The fries will already be salted, but should I bring vinegar with the order?"

He smiled. "You remembered what we talked about last night."

"I did, yeah." She looked pleased. "Vinegar, then?"

"I'd love that."

"Thought so." She hurried away.

"I'd forgotten about the salt and vinegar on fries. I'm a catsup girl all the way."

He shuddered. "I can't imagine how that tastes."

"Then you should try it. Today. I can't let you go home without eating at least one fry dipped in catsup."

"It sounds godawful. Looks that way, too."

"Says the man whose country invented haggis."

"For the record, I don't eat haggis."

"No? What kind of a Highlander are you, then?"

"The non-haggis eatin' kind."

"And the powers-that-be let you get away with that?"

"I don't go around announcin' it."

"You just did."

"To you. I don't announce it back home."

"Why not?"

"I'd be askin' for some haggis-eating Scotsman to insist he can teach me to like it. I don't want to create that challenge for any of my countrymen and women. They'd fail and I'd feel like a turncoat."

"Goodness. That seems like a truly weighty problem."

"Aye. Ranks right up there with solving the mystery of black holes. It did occur to me that you might have chosen *Ring of Fire* to honor your black hole research and not to celebrate my embarrassin' encounter with Ellie Mae."

"No, it was all about you and Ellie Mae."

"And how could you resist? The image of me shopping for condoms with the help of an eighty-something woman must have been too temptin' to ignore."

"Yep."

"They'd better be all that she promised, too." He took a sip of his water. He was stalling because he didn't want to go into this. They were having such a bonnie time...

"Rory, what is it?"

"A bloody difficult topic."

"I had a feeling. You've had tells all over the place."

"And that's why I'd never play poker with anyone, unless it was strip poker with you."

She gazed at him. "You don't want to play poker with me."

"I believe you." She had the greenest eyes. He liked that she'd chosen to wear her glasses instead of contacts for this outing, as if she wanted him to see her real self. "We've established you're much smarter than I am. Then again, if my goal was to lose that game, I'd be all in."

Her cheeks flushed. "How you talk."

"Maybe we should go back to Pills and Pop and buy a pack of cards. I'll bet they have—"

"You're avoiding the issue."

He sighed and leaned back in his chair. "So I am." What a damn mess. "I had a phone conversation with my brother Aleck today."

"When did you talk with him?"

"While you were in the shower."

"And?"

"Catriona and her father are threatenin' to sue me for breach of promise. By leavin' the country, I made myself look guilty. Aleck is ready to fight for me, but for that to be effective, I need to go home."

"When?"

"He recommended comin' as soon as possible, so he can document everything leadin' up to this point. He wants me to book a flight out tomorrow if I could find one with an empty seat."

"Oh." The flash of dismay in her eyes warmed his heart. But she doused it immediately. "You should do whatever you need to do."

"That's not as easy as it sounds."

"Why not? You're being attacked and you need to defend yourself. It's a no-brainer."

"But it means leavin' you. We'd only have a short time to—"

"I know what it means. I never expected a happily-ever-after with you, so what difference does it make to us if you leave tomorrow or a week from tomorrow? No matter how you slice it, we still have an expiration date."

<u>15</u>

Damaris refused to allow her disappointment to show. So what if their affair had shrunk from approximately a week to one afternoon and night? Time was relative. One night or one week. Still finite.

"I haven't said I would go."

"We both know that's the best course of action. You need to save the career you love. In your shoes, I'd go back."

"Here we are!" Jenny appeared, all smiles, with two foaming mugs of ale and two orders of crisp fries. "Bon appetite!"

"Thanks so much, Jenny." Damaris did her best to return Jenny's smile.

"What in blue blazes happened here?" Jenny glanced from Damaris to Rory. "I leave two happy people and come back to the most down-in-the-mouth couple I've seen in the GG for months. What's the deal?"

"I might have to leave tomorrow," Rory said. "I'm needed back home."

"But you just got here!"

"I know, but there's a bit of a guddle that has to be handled."

"A guddle?" Jenny looked puzzled.

"Aye. In other words, a mess."

"What a wonderful word! I'm adopting it for my own. But I hate that you have a guddle that will take you away so soon. Isn't there any way to handle it from here?"

Damaris had picked up her mug of ale, ready to drown her sorrows, but she put it back down. She'd accepted this turn of events without firing a shot. Had she given up too easily?

Jenny balanced her tray on her hip. "I mean, we have all sorts of ways to connect these days—phones, email, even face-to-face chats online. Surely—"

"Jenny, you're brilliant." Damaris exchanged a glance with Rory. "That just might work."

He gave a slow nod. "I see where you're goin' with this, lass. It could at least buy some time."

"It could." Damn it, she *had* given up too easily. Checked her brain at the door when her emotions had become involved. "Thank you, Jenny."

"Glad to be of help. Next time either of you end up with a guddle, let me know." She grinned and walked away.

Damaris looked across the table at Rory. "This could be the solution that satisfies everyone." Especially her. And that, damn it, was important, too. "If Aleck needs documentation, he can record a video chat with you. That would be a faster, more efficient way for him to compile what he needs, anyway."

"If he agrees to it. I think part of me goin' back is symbolic."

"You will go back, but why does the opposition have to know exactly when?"

"That's a good point. When are you leavin'?"

"My flight's on Saturday morning."

"Then I'll fly out Saturday, too. That's assumin' Aleck goes along with this alternative."

"Why not? A chance to spend time with your Montana relatives doesn't come along every day. No telling when you'll be back to see them again. Forcing you to leave when there's a reasonable alternative would be—"

"He knows that wouldn't be the whole reason."

She blinked. "What do you mean?"

"I told him about you."

"You *what*?"

"When he asked me to come home right away, I started hedgin'. Talked about how much I was enjoyin' the visit with our cousins. He asked if there was a woman involved."

Her stomach churned. "Why would he do that?"

"He knows me well enough to pick up somethin' in my tone."

"Does he hear that something in your tone often, then?"

"No, lass, he doesn't." He reached across the table and took her hand in both of his. Then he lowered his voice. "I don't blame you for thinkin' that, since I'm here because of that situation with Catriona and now you and I have...plans."

"I shouldn't care if you've had a string of lovers a mile long."

"But I think you do. I see it in your eyes."

"I'm the one who mentioned having an affair."

"And I'm the one who said I didn't want to start somethin' that would have to end in a week. I haven't had a string of lovers. Ladies do seem to like me, but I don't play fast and loose with them."

She took a shaky breath. "I'm going to choose to believe that."

"Please do."

"What does your brother know about me?"

"That you're a hard-workin' theoretical physicist who's taking her first vacation in four years. And that I'm honored to be the man who'll be allowed to share it with you."

"And what does he think of that?"

"He's hopin' I'll cut my visit short, which would reduce the chance of me gettin' into another guddle."

"Then when you talk to him again, please assure him there will be no guddle. I understand the parameters. You'll go back to the distillery career you're excited about, the one you've trained for and I'll go back to investigating black holes. We'll think of each other fondly. End of story."

"You said we'd keep in touch."

Like this? He hadn't released her hand, and he'd begun stroking the inside of her wrist with his thumb. His gaze had gone all warm and mellow, too.

She cleared her throat. "We can keep in touch, but realistically, with me being in California and you being in Scotland, it'll be by email, mostly."

"I'm imaginin' somethin' a bit more personal."

"Oh?" Her heart thumped faster. "Like what?"

"You said you wanted to keep your connection to this place, and so do I. In that context, *keepin' in touch* might mean you'd let me know the dates of your visit in case I could schedule a trip over at the same time."

"What exactly are you talking about?"

He smiled. "I don't want to lose the connection to this place...or to you."

"So you really don't want an affair."

He shook his head. "Neither do you."

"You can see into my head?"

"I can see into your heart."

Now her breathing was wonky. "That might be...the most romantic thing anyone has ever...said to me."

"Then I'm glad I said it."

Jenny whisked by on her way to another table. "Much better. Much, much better."

Damaris looked at their joined hands. "We won't be able to drink our beer this way."

He grinned. "That might be the most unromantic thing anyone has ever said to me."

She smiled back. "Yeah, well, I'm a scientist. Deal with it."

"Gladly." He gave her hand a squeeze, let go and picked up his beer mug. "To keepin' in touch."

"To keeping in touch." She tapped her mug against his. "Whatever that means."

"That's up to us."

"I vote for whatever makes us happy."

"I'll drink to that, too." He sipped his ale. "Nice. Do they brew it here?"

"Not that I know of. Wouldn't that require a dedicated space, a relatively large one?"

"Aye."

"They don't have that, so they must purchase their beer elsewhere."

"It's good, in any case." He put down his mug and picked up the bottle of white vinegar Jenny had brought with the order.

"Wait. Don't put that on yet. To make this a true test, you need to take a fry and dip it in catsup before you sprinkle on the vinegar."

"Damn. I thought you'd forgotten."

"I don't generally forget things."

"That's something we have in common, then. The memory of puttin' that disgusting red stuff in my mouth will follow me to the grave."

"Don't be such a baby. It's catsup, not arsenic." She moved her fries over on the plate, grabbed the bottle and created a small dipping puddle in the vacant spot. "There you go." She pushed her plate in his direction. "And don't be a wimp. Shove it all the way in."

"I love it when you talk dirty."

She rolled her eyes. "Boys."

He laughed. "Girls." Then he made a great show of submerging the fry in the catsup. Eventually he lifted it for her inspection. "Good enough?"

"Yes. Now eat it."

He squeezed his eyes shut, opened his mouth and popped the fry inside. Keeping his eyes closed tight, he chewed and swallowed before slowly opening his eyes again.

"Well? That wasn't so bad, was it?"

"It was worse. That's the slimiest fry I've ever had in my entire life."

"Slimy? How can you say that? Did you even taste it or did you put it so far back on your tongue that you couldn't tell how sweet and delicious catsup is?"

"There's no such thing as too far back. That's a misconception. Your entire tongue can detect everything—salty, sour, bitter, sweet and savory."

"Is that so?"

"Aye." His eyebrows lifted. "Have I hit on a wee bit of information you don't know?"

"You have. I'm no expert on taste buds. Sounds like you might be."

"If you want to make top-notch single malt, you'd better learn how tongues work, although your nose is more important in determinin' how something tastes."

"I knew that. When you have a cold, things don't taste right, or they have no flavor at all."

"Your brain's involved, too. It's a three-way operation. In this case, my brain, my nose and my tongue agree that catsup is nasty."

"One man's opinion." She dipped a fry in the catsup and put it in her mouth. Then she closed her eyes as if savoring the experience and deliberately moaned with pleasure. A sharp intake of breath startled her and she quickly opened her eyes.

Heat flickered in Rory's gaze. "That got to me, lass."

"Oh." She gulped. "I was just goofing around. I didn't think of what it might sound like." But she was thinking about it, now.

He picked up his beer mug and his hand shook slightly. He took several long swallows before he set the mug on the table. "That's better."

"Sorry."

"Don't be." He sprinkled vinegar on his fries. "I seem to have an overactive imagination where you're concerned."

"This is new for me."

"New?"

"I don't normally affect a man this strongly. I'm not deliberately trying to stir you up."

"I think that's part of it." He began eating his fries.

"I don't know what you mean."

He finished chewing and swallowed. "You seem to have no idea how sexy you are."

"Sexy? Me?"

"You have this one thing you do, when you lift your hair off the back of your neck, and your breasts shift slightly under your shirt. My mouth goes dry every time."

She stared at him, pulse racing. "I...um...do that because my hair's thick and I want to...catch a breeze."

"And you catch me, too. In that moment, I become your willing slave."

She could barely breathe. Her soft voice didn't sound anything like her. "I've never had a willing slave in my life."

"You have one, now."

<u>16</u>

Rory hadn't wanted a woman this much since...hell, he'd never wanted a woman this much. Or had so many hurdles to leap before he could do something about it.

He managed to change the tone of the conversation so he and Damaris could finish their ale and fries. He asked about the only cousin he didn't have a handle on and learned that Trevor worked construction and was also a volunteer firefighter. He and Olivia, an accountant, hadn't announced a date yet but everyone expected them to marry soon.

"I think I have all the McGavins straight," he said as he drove back to Wild Creek Ranch. "So it's on to the Sawyers. After the foalin' I won't forget Wes or what he does for a livin'. I know who Roxanne is. But your spreadsheet listed Quinn with four kids. Who're the other two?"

"Pete, the oldest, and Gage, the next oldest. Pete's the foreman at a guest ranch outside of town and Gage hired on at the raptor rescue center. If we go there this week—"

"That's a priority. I don't want to leave without seein' that place. Aleck has to see reason on this situation."

"What time is it there?"

He consulted the dashboard clock. "Ten-thirty. He might still be awake, but I'd rather not present this idea when he's tired. Or out havin' drinks with friends. I promised to call him in the mornin' at quarter-to-five our time. I'll stick to that."

"Let's think positive, that he'll go along with a change of plans."

"I'm for that." He glanced over at her. "Are you ready to give me a ridin' lesson?"

Her cheeks turned a soft shade of pink. "Is that what we're calling it?"

"As far as Cody and Zane are concerned, it is. I asked Kendra about a potential horseback ride and she was goin' to alert her boys that we'd be comin' down to the barn."

"I asked her about it before we left, too, so they should be well alerted."

"I figure they'll saddle Diablo for me. Will you get Fifty Shades?"

"I doubt it. They borrowed that dapple gray from Crimson Clouds, where Pete works. The horses on loan have likely been returned. I'm happy with any horse they give me. They're all sweethearts."

"Except Licorice, evidently."

"Nobody will be riding her anytime soon. It's best to wait until Eclipse is weaned."

"When's that?"

"Sometime around seven or eight months."

"That's another reason I want to stay until the end of the week. Kendra said they'll let Eclipse out in the pasture after a few days. I want to see his first glimpse of the outside world." He rounded a bend in the ranch road. The house was straight ahead. "Do you need to go back inside for any reason?"

"You can drive straight to the barn. I'm sure there's an old hat in the tack room I can borrow. I'd like to stay out of the house and give Kendra and Quinn some privacy."

He smiled. "For their lie-down?"

"Yeah. I love the way they look at each other, as if they can't believe their good luck."

"I want to tell ma and da about that, because last they heard, she was still on her own. They'll be happy for her."

"See how valuable this trip has been as a bridge between the Scottish and the American McGavins? What a shame if you didn't stay a little longer."

"Exactly. I'll add that to my list of reasons to give my brother tomorrow. Where should I park down here?"

"Over by Zane's pickup."

"If I could stay longer, I'd want to try drivin' a pickup. This little car isn't right for cowboy country."

"No, it's not." There was a smile in her voice. "I think you're growing fond of this place."

"I know I am. I didn't think I'd like it this much. And yes, you have somethin' to do with that, but it's also the good-natured spirit of this ranch and the town. Relaxed and friendly. Hopeful. I'll need to come back every now and then just to soak that up."

"Me, too." She opened her door the minute he turned off the motor. "Before we go out for a ride, let's peek in on Eclipse."

"You can go ahead. I need to take care of somethin'."

"What?"

"Transferrin' my purchase to my pocket."

"I can wait."

"I'm tryin' to be subtle, lass."

"Oh. Okay. I'll just go on in, then."

"Good." After he levered himself out of the driver's side, he reached behind the seat for the bag from Pills and Pop. He took out the box, opened it and shoved two condoms in his front pocket.

Then he gazed at the plastic bag. Might come in handy. Folding it into a tight square, he tucked it in his other front pocket.

Other than that, he'd have to play this by ear. He was primarily a city boy, aside from the times he'd stayed overnight at his gran and grandpa's farm. He'd been too young for this activity back then.

He was used to inside sex, which usually involved a bed. Didn't have to, but often did. He was counting on Damaris to know the ropes on this one.

The barn door was open and he left it that way when he walked into the barn. The aroma was slightly different from his days at the sheep farm, but the earthy scent appealed to him just as much.

The barn was warmer than it had been in the early morning hours. Quieter, too. A soft buzz of conversation drifted from the area in front of Licorice's stall, where Damaris stood talking with Zane and admiring the foal.

As Rory started down the aisle to join them, he passed empty stalls. In the crisp light of pre-dawn, horses had stood munching hay from mesh contraptions hooked to the wall. Damaris had told him what they were called. Hay nets? That sounded right.

But he wasn't talking cowboy yet and he certainly hadn't mastered the cowboy way. He wasn't clear on the concept by any means. He needed more time with Quinn and Kendra. More time with Damaris. More time.

He approached Licorice's stall. "How're they doin'?"

"Hey, Rory." Zane turned to shake hands with him. "They're doing super. Both sleeping. Take my spot and I'll head out to the pasture to catch Diablo and Jake."

"If it's all right with you, I'd like to help with that, learn how it's done."

"Sure thing. I'll fetch a couple of lead ropes and meet you by the door."

"Thanks. Appreciate it." He moved into Zane's place beside Damaris.

She glanced at him. "You dive right in, don't you?"

"Aye. Especially when I'm short on time." He gazed down at Licorice and Eclipse, cuddled together like interlocked puzzle pieces as they slept. Eclipse's coat was a lighter shade of brown now that it was dry. Softer looking. "I can't believe he was born this morning. He already looks older."

"Because he's all dried off and fluffy. Zane said he's almost mastered getting up. Doesn't fall much at all. If the weather holds, they'll take him out to the pasture Wednesday or Thursday."

"I have to be here."

"I agree. It's like watching a baby's first steps. I wouldn't miss it for the world."

"Nor will I." He stepped away and tugged on the brim of his hat. "Let's go catch some horses."

Zane was waiting with two lead ropes and a battered brown hat. He handed a rope to each of them and gave Damaris the hat. She settled it on her head.

The transformation into a cowgirl was instant and adorable. An intellectual cowgirl, at that. He was a fan.

"You know what, Rory? You don't need me out there teaching you if you have Damaris. She's a good hand. She'll show you how it's done. I'll go back to mucking out stalls."

"Is that what I think it is?"

Zane grinned. "If you're picturing a shovel, a rake and manure, you're on target."

"I'd like to take a turn at that, too."

"Now?"

"Maybe not this very minute, but soon. I expect you muck out stalls every day."

"Someone does. Not always me. And not usually this late. Between the wedding and the foal, the schedule's out of whack. If you show up around nine in the morning, Cody will be here and he'd welcome the help."

"If there are enough shovels and rakes," Damaris said, "I'll be here, too."

"We can always scare up extra shovels and rakes." Zane looked amused. "But Mom said you were on vacation this week. Wouldn't you rather lounge on the porch with a good book?"

"You'll laugh, but I've missed mucking out stalls."

"Yeah, that makes me laugh." He thumbed back his hat. "But I get it. There's a reason I keep working here and hire assistants over at Raptors Rise. Financially I could make the rescue operation my full-time job, but then I wouldn't be interacting with horses every day."

"I've never known what that's like," Damaris said. "I got out here as often as I could once I could drive myself, but this is the first time I've stayed overnight. I'm a little jealous of you guys."

"Come more often, then. Mom would love it."

"I would, too. I'll see how it goes. Well, we're burning daylight, Rory. Gotta catch those ponies and saddle up or we'll have a very short ride."

"Lead the way." He fell into step beside her as they walked out to the pasture. "Been thinkin' about what Jenny said. How everyone can be virtually connected these days."

"And?"

"I don't pretend to know what your job is like, but could you do any of it remotely so you could live here most of the time?"

"At the ranch? I would never impose on Kendra like—"

"Not here, I guess, but nearby, so you could be part of ranch life."

"It's a beautiful fantasy, but the point of working on the Caltech campus is the constant interaction with other top-drawer scientists."

"Like a think tank?"

"Exactly."

"Couldn't you create a virtual think tank?"

"I don't know. Maybe. But part of what I love about staying on this ranch is the ambiance— the log ranch house with the massive fireplace, being able to walk to the barn or the pasture anytime I want. I love *this*." She spread her arms to include everything in sight. "Short of living with Kendra, which I doubt either of us would go for, I couldn't move to Eagles Nest and replicate my experience here."

"Guess not. I see what you mean." Her reasoning was sound and it put the lid on some crazy fantasies he'd had, that she'd move over here and he'd manage to visit often enough to …what? Have a workable relationship?

Nay. He and Damaris were sharing a temporary dream that would be over at the end of the week.

Damaris touched his arm. "Thanks for the thought, though."

"You just sounded so wistful when you were talkin' with Zane. And you look great in that hat."

"Thanks." She sighed. "I probably sounded wistful because my research isn't going well. Living on this ranch looks way more fun than my life in California."

"It also looks way more fun than bein' jobless in Scotland and dealin' with a nasty woman and her father."

She unlatched the gate. "See? No wonder we're charmed by Wild Creek. Once we go home and deal with our problems, we'll see this for what it is, a lovely experience that doesn't fit with our real lives."

"I suppose." He followed her into the pasture and latched the gate behind him. "But I still want to learn everythin' I can about bein' a cowboy."

"Then here's your first tip. We're in a horse pasture. Watch your step."

"I'm not completely clueless." The battered hat looked perfect on her. She might not believe that she belonged here, but he couldn't shake the image of her riding horses and wearing that hat. "I've walked through sheep pastures before."

"But sheep droppings are different."

"Aye, but you still have to watch out." How an old hat could make her look even sexier was hard to explain, but she...wait. What was that squishing sound? He lifted his boot. "Bloody hell."

<u>17</u>

Damaris hid a smile as Rory scraped his boot on a clump of thick grass.

"Feel free to say *I told you so.* I deserve it."

"Think of this as part of your initiation."

He glanced up and flashed her a grin. "That's a good way of lookin' at it, lass. I learn by doin'. This won't happen twice."

"I believe you. I spotted Diablo over there." She pointed him out.

"I see him."

"Take it slow and easy. As you walk up to him, chose an angle that lets him see you. Horses are prey animals, so they get nervous if someone approaches them from behind."

"Can I try somethin' first?"

"Like what?"

"Like this." He stuck his tongue behind his teeth and let out a sharp whistle.

Diablo lifted his head, looked at Rory and ambled over.

"How did you know to do that?"

"Quinn mentioned that Diablo responds to a whistle. He was trained to do it before Kendra got him. I wasn't sure if it would work since he doesn't know me like he knows Quinn." Rory stroked the gelding's nose and scratched behind his ears. "Now that I've got him, what's next?"

"Clip the lead rope to his halter so you can lead him through the gate and over to the hitching post."

"All right."

"I'll fetch Jake. I could whistle all day long and he wouldn't come. Be right back." She walked up to the big bay. "Did you see that, Jake? I'll bet I could train you to come when I whistle. Except I can't whistle through my teeth like some people."

"I could teach you," Rory called over.

"You've got a deal!" She clipped the rope to Jake's halter and stroked his neck. "Let's go, big guy."

Rory stopped stroking Diablo and turned toward her. "You're walking on his left. Is that the best way to do it?"

"It's the most common. That's likely what Diablo's used to."

"Then that's how we'll do it, Diablo. Just how you like it." He took hold of the rope in his right hand and held the end loosely in his left as he started toward her.

He made quite a picture leading that gelding like a seasoned hand. Took her breath away. Long before she'd fallen for Jamie Fraser, she'd had a thing for cowboys. A cowboy with a brogue made an irresistible combination.

He paused. "Am I doin' somethin' wrong?"

"Not at all. Why?"

"You were starin' at me like maybe I was."

"I was staring because you look great, as if you were born to work with horses."

"Funny you should say that. I'm beginnin' to think I was. I'll go first and open the gate."

"Sure." Gave her more opportunity to drink in the sight of him. Lordy.

Moments later the horses stood quietly at the hitching post while she took Rory though the basics of saddling and bridling. He was a quick study. Didn't take long before they were ready to mount up.

She supervised him as he climbed aboard. "You've got that part down."

"Mountin' is easy for me, now. It's the ridin' where I struggle. Can't sit a trot worth a damn."

"That's okay. We can work on it. Let me tell Zane we're taking off." She walked up to the barn door. "We're leaving! We'll be gone about..." She turned toward Rory and lifted her eyebrows.

He shrugged.

"See you in a couple of hours!"

"Okay," Zane called back. "I might be gone by then. Have fun!"

"We will!"

Behind her, Rory's soft chuckle sent a shiver of anticipation up her spine. Until that moment, she'd submerged their ultimate plan under a flurry of preparation for the ride. Otherwise she would have been all thumbs. But now...

She turned and looked at him sitting easily in the saddle. "Ready?"

"More than ready. I'm hopin' there's a good place not too far."

"There is if it's still there. The trail is narrow, more of a game trail, really. We'll have to keep the horses down to a walk. But you can practice your skills just fine—heels down, lower back loose and spine in easy alignment."

"I'll do my best."

With a quick nod, she swung up on Jake. "Follow me." She rode toward a much simpler gate, one with only a loop of wire to hold it closed.

Once there, she reached down, opened it and motioned him through. She followed on Jake, repositioned the loop and turned to Rory. "This way." She pointed to her right. "We'll have to ride single file."

"Following you is a pleasure. Fuels my imagination."

She met his gaze. Holy smoldering lust. No man had ever looked at her with enough heat to melt her panties. Her hands trembled on the reins. "Let's go."

About ten yards from the gate, the trail dipped into the trees. "Low-hanging branches. Watch your head."

"Got it."

She hadn't ridden this trail since high school, but it had been one of her favorites when she'd taken solo rides. The small glen was only about ten minutes away, assuming it hadn't become overgrown since she'd last been there.

Only the chirp of birds and the steady clop of hooves broke the silence. The rapid thudding of her heart sounded loud to her, but that didn't mean he could hear it. Was his beating like that, too? She bet it was.

The glen should be coming up. Lifting in the saddle, she peered through the trees. Was it still there? Yes! She turned back to him. "We're in luck. My little hideaway spot looks about the same."

"Yours?"

"Not really. I call it that, but—"

"Mind your head, lass!"

She swung around just in time to duck. "Whew. Thanks."

"You might be a wee bit distracted."

"You think?"

"I almost whacked my noggin a while ago."

"Then it's a good thing we're here." She rode into the small clearing and dismounted. "My favorite spot."

"Thank the Lord." He winced as he swung down from the saddle.

"Oh, no!" She dropped Jake's reins to the ground and hurried to him. "Did you hurt yourself riding?"

His smile was tight. "I dinna think how ridin' would squeeze my tadger."

Evidently his brogue was more pronounced when he was aroused. She could guess the meaning of tadger from a quick glance below his belt. "I, um, didn't think of that. Do you need to..."

"Aye, I need to." He dropped Diablo's reins to the ground. "Will the horses be—"

"Fine. They'll munch some grass."

"Good." He took off his hat, hung it on the saddle horn and reached for her. "Been thinkin' about kissin' ye since last night. Dreamed about—" He paused and lifted off her hat. "This has to go."

She quivered. "Doesn't everything have to go?"

"Sure and it does." He propped her hat on top of his. "But first, kiss me, afore I go half-crazy with wantin' the touch of your mouth."

Shoving her glasses to the top of her head, she nestled against him and cupped the back of his neck. "You sound very Scottish right now."

"Canna help it. Hope you dunna mind."

"On the contrary." She urged him closer and met him halfway. "I love it." Then she gave him an open-mouthed kiss that ought to tell him everything he needed to know.

It must have worked because he groaned and took the kiss deeper, making love to her mouth with such abandon that she nearly climaxed. She wriggled away, gasping. "Rory! I'm dying, here!"

"So am I, lass." Panting, he stripped off his shirt and laid it on the ground. "Lie on this."

Sweetest gesture in the world. "I will, but first I should take off a few things."

"I'll help ye."

Dear God, his thickened accent was nearly as exciting as his gentle hands lifting off her glasses, easing her shirt free and unhooking her bra.

After setting everything on the ground near his shirt, he straightened, cupped her breasts and leaned down to lightly kiss the tip of each. "So bonnie," he murmured. "So verra bonnie." Without warning, he lifted her in his arms and laid her down on the shirt he'd spread out.

She squeaked in surprise. "But I still have on my boots! And my jeans! And my—"

"'Tis not important. Dunna worry. Just let me kiss ye here…and here…and here…"

She ran up the white flag. His mouth roamed her hot, trembling body, setting off mini-explosions of delight as he sucked, nipped, nuzzled and licked.

Delirious with pleasure, she lost track of the sequence of events. Somehow he divested her of her boots. Then her jeans were gone, which exposed more territory for him to explore. He seemed to know when a breeze had cooled her damp skin and he returned to that spot to sip and suckle until she pulsed with urgency.

"Rory." Her voice was hoarse. "I want…I need…" Coherence was lost. Rational thought was gone. She ached with a fierce passion that had no name. "*Please.*"

"Aye." Ragged breathing telegraphed that she wasn't the only one beside herself. "'Tis time." Taking his warmth with him, he sat nearby and pulled off his boots. Then he stood and unzipped his jeans.

She looked up as he stripped off both jeans and briefs. Then she gulped. Maybe it was the angle, but…no, not the angle. Wow. Just wow.

He fished in the pocket of his jeans and came up with a square packet. She hated to see him cover up that work of art. She would have liked to admire it a little longer.

Except every second he was away ramped up the tension building in the epicenter of her restless body. She'd always believed that sexual desire was a predictable result of replicable stimuli. She'd dare anyone to replicate this moment.

Kneeling beside her, Rory leaned down and placed a soft kiss on her lips. Then he lifted his head and gazed into her eyes. "Can ye see me?"

"Yes." She dragged in air. "I'm near-sighted."

"Wanted to make sure, because there's somethin' I need to say, even if holdin' back is causin' me to shake. And I need ye to see my face when I say it."

She slid both hands up his cheeks, which were scratchy with the beginnings of his beard. "I can see your face, Rory."

"Then here 'tis. I've never known anyone like ye, Damaris. I think…nay, I *know* we have somethin' special. I dunna understand what that means, or where this is goin'. But 'tis not a temporary diversion."

"I believe you."

"Good. If ye dinna understand, I'd—"

"Get dressed?"

"Nay. Might not have the willpower when I'm so close. But I'd not be lovin' ye quite the same if ye dinna believe me."

She gazed into those blue eyes and her heart swelled with excitement. "Then give it all you've got."

He moved over her. "I'll ask the same of ye, lass."

<u>**18**</u>

Making love was never ordinary. But making love to Damaris would forever change her life and his. Rory had wanted to make sure she understood that, even a wee bit, before proceeding.

He would have proceeded anyway because he was a lusty Scotsman and his tadger ached something fierce. But he would have held back as much of himself as possible. Thank God he didn't have to.

She was all in, rising to meet him as he thrust deep into her warm, receptive body. Ah, sweet heaven, he'd been right! Locked in snug and secure, he gazed down at her, searching her bright eyes for what he longed to find.

Yes. There it was. Recognition. His heart swelled. "See what I mean, lass?"

She nodded.

Slowly he began to move. "I canna make promises."

Her breath came faster. "Neither can I."

"But this...'tis...I canna put words to it."

"Don't try." She wrapped him in her arms and held on tight. "Just be here with me."

He'd never been more present in his life. Each stroke, each magical time he settled deep in her willing body, he forged another link binding them together more surely than words said before a preacher.

His nostrils filled with the scent of crushed grass, evergreen and musk. Bird song blended with her soft gasps, his rough breathing and the rhythmic, liquid sound of lovemaking.

He saw only her—green eyes dark as rain-dampened moss, lips red from his kisses, cheeks flushed pink. Her generous breasts, tipped with burgundy, shivered with each thrust.

He moved faster and her fingertips dug into his back. Then she began to pant, squeezed his tadger and cried out his name. She was coming, recklessly surrendering all that she was. To him.

With a groan wrenched from the depths of his soul, he gave in kind. Surging forward, he poured himself into her with a fierce rush that made his ears ring. Braced above her, he gulped for air as the waves of her climax rippled over his still-hard tadger.

He gazed into her eyes as the ripples slowly subsided. He didn't want to blink, didn't want to miss a second of the emotion shining there. Didn't want to move and shatter the perfection of being intimately joined.

Her soft mouth tilted in a smile. Reaching up, she stroked his cheek. "We can't stay like this forever."

"Why not?"

"Physics."

He laughed. Dear God, that felt good. She laughed, too, and her breasts jiggled. He balanced on one forearm so he could touch her there. "You're a gift, lass."

"You're an entire room full of presents."

"I'm glad you think so." He sighed. "You're right about movin', though. There's a sharp rock under my knee. Didn't feel it until now."

"There's also one under my tush."

"Damn." He carefully disengaged and moved back. "I should've checked the ground before I—"

"Checked the ground? Do you not remember how frantic we were?"

"Aye." He stood, grabbed his jeans and pulled a handkerchief from the back pocket and the plastic bag from the front.

"You lapsed into saying things like *ye* and *'tis*." She sat up. "Which I adored by the way."

He chuckled. "When I start talkin' like that you'll know I'm either aroused or drunk."

"That's good intel." She stood. "Getting drunk is bad for your liver, but I'll happily keep you aroused so I can hear that thick brogue some more."

"Stroll around like that and you'll achieve your aim in no time." Once he'd dealt with the condom he allowed himself to fully enjoy the sight of Damaris, gloriously naked and...wearing her glasses? "Why'd you put those back on?"

"The better to view your tadger."

He grinned. "You've expanded your vocabulary."

"Yes, and that's my new favorite word." Her glance drifted downward. "On the other hand, I forgot to ask how many condoms you put in your pocket."

"I might have brought a spare."

"Oh?" Her gaze lifted and her eyes sparkled. "Just in case you enjoyed yourself the first time?"

"Just in case." He drew closer and took her by the shoulders. "But I'll not have you gettin' bruised again. Let me see your backside." He turned her gently around and crouched down. "Ah, lass, ye have a wee bruise." He kissed the faint bluish spot. Then he licked it.

She sucked in a breath. "Are you making it better?"

"Aye." He kissed and nuzzled her silken bottom. Then he slid his hand between her damp thighs to caress his tadger's favorite place. "I dunna want ye lyin' on the ground this time. I'll take the ground. Ye will take the top."

Her reply was breathy. "Sounds like fun."

"Mm-hm." He nibbled his way up the curve of her spine, lifted her thick hair and pressed his mouth against her nape. Her breast filled his hand, her nipple taut between his fingers.

She moaned, and the depth of yearning in the sound went straight to his groin. Circling her hips, he pulled her against his aroused body and put his lips next to her ear. "Dunna want to let you go."

She trembled. "If you...want to lie down, I'll get the condom."

"Front pocket."

"I know."

He gave her ear a gentle nip. "Be verra quick."

"I will."

Releasing her, he knelt beside his shirt, located the rock and removed it. Then he stretched out on his back.

"Found it."

"I see that." A naked beauty holding a condom would make any man's staff snap to attention. His was no exception.

She sank to her knees beside him. "I'll do it." She ripped open the packet and gazed at his tadger. "I hate to cover it up."

"Then let me—"

"But I will." Pushing her glasses to the top of her head, she leaned over him. As she rolled on the condom, her breasts swayed gently.

He closed his eyes. If he watched her, he'd explode for sure. But that left nothing to distract him from the erotic brush of her fingers.

Her warm breath feathered his cheek. "Done." And she kissed him.

He would never get enough of her mouth. Sliding his hands through her luxurious hair, he held her head and kissed her back. Yes, he wanted all the rest, and soon, but her kiss was full of joy and he wanted more...and even more...

She dragged her mouth away, gasping. "I've never known a man who kisses like you. I was completely satisfied a while ago and now I want you again. What's that about?"

"Chemistry."

"Smarty pants."

"Not wearin' any."

Her gaze traveled over him again, more slowly. "I really like you without pants."

"I really like ye without 'em, too."

She swallowed. "I'm not used to...wanting someone with such...urgency. I'm feeling a little...out of control."

"As am I." He reached for her hand. "'Tis a good thing."

"Scary, though."

"Nay." He squeezed her hand. "Come to me, lass."

"Gladly." She straddled his thighs. Slowly her mouth tilted at the corners. Spreading her fingers, she planted both hands on his chest. "Permission to come aboard, sir."

"Permission granted. I'll guide ye." He grasped her hips and lifted her into position.

"I want to look." She dipped her head to glance backward, obscuring his view.

He could do this blindfolded, but her hair tickled his chest, adding one more delicious sensation to test his restraint as he lowered her slowly.

Lifting her head, she met his gaze as he completed the connection. Emotion flared in the green depths of her eyes. She swallowed. "The first time was...so good."

His chest heaved. "Aye."

"This will be better."

19

Rory's powerful chest, rising and falling with his labored breathing, was a lovely place for Damaris to rest her hands. His light dusting of dark red hair was springy beneath her palms. Best of all, his rapid heartbeat vibrated under her fingertips.

Down below, he filled her completely, anchoring her so securely that she wasn't sure if she could move. Wasn't sure if she wanted to when he thrust upward ever so slightly, setting off a quiver that promised future delights.

She loved being connected to him, loved staring into his blue eyes, especially when he looked at her like this, as if he saw her as the most beautiful and desirable woman in the world. No man had done that before.

She eased upward, relishing the tantalizing friction. A muscle in his jaw tightened. "Too much?"

"Ye must...let me catch my breath. Dunna want to come yet."

His thick brogue thrilled her to her toes. "Me, either."

He grasped her hips more firmly. "Now, lass. Easy up and easy down."

She smiled. "Are you asking me to be gentle?"

His answering smile was a little strained. "When I tighten my grip, stop."

"I will." She eased upward. Mm. Nice. His fingers pressed harder. She paused, then slid back down. "How's that?"

"Good. Again. Faster."

She followed his directions and he gasped. "Too fast?"

"Too good." He drew in a breath, expanding his massive chest. "Ne'er been like this. I could come just lookin' at ye."

Pleasure rippled through her, centering in her core. "Keep talking like that and I'll come, too."

"Should've brought three." He took several deep breaths. "Again. A wee bit slower. There. Good. Like that."

She moved in a lazy rhythm as tension gradually built in her core. His breathing grew ragged. Hers, too. Oh, my, he'd shifted his hand. His thumb was circling, pressing…

"Slower." His muttered command was followed by a deep groan.

"No." She flattened her palms against his sweaty chest and went for it, glorying in the intense friction, his bellow of release…and an orgasm that roared through her like a tsunami.

He lay there panting, his eyes closed. "Thank you, lass."

She placed a kiss on his warm chest. "For being gentle with you?"

"For lettin' me love you." He opened his eyes and held her gaze. "It's a rare privilege."

The words poured over her in a glittering shower of splendor. Her throat tightened. "What a beautiful thing to say."

"What a beautiful woman to say it to."

"Much more of that and I'm liable to tear up."

He stroked her cheek. "I wouldn't mind."

"I would. I refuse to let this incredible afternoon end in tears, even if they are happy ones."

He smiled. "Is it endin', then?"

"Guess so. We need to get the horses back to the barn. It's feeding time. And dinnertime soon after at the ranch."

He sighed. "And I look forward to that. Except…"

"Except?"

"I'm greedy. I want more time alone with you. Doin' this."

"We'll figure it out."

"Promise?"

"Rory, I would be a fool not to spend every single minute I can with you. Trust me, I'll be looking for opportunities like this."

"That's all I needed to hear. Now I'm ready to go back. And I'll tell Kendra tonight about the mess I left in Scotland."

"Like I said, she'll be understanding."

"I'll cling to that thought, lass."

* * *

With only four of them at dinner, Kendra had set two places on one side of the long table and two on the other. She and Quinn sat together and so did Damaris and Rory. The setup couldn't have been more perfect for either Kendra or Quinn to notice a change in the dynamic.

Damaris waited, anticipating that first comment. Surely one of them would see that she wasn't the same person who'd eaten breakfast with them this morning.

Yes, she'd cleaned up a bit, put on a little makeup and brushed her hair. She didn't look quite as ravished as she had when she'd first walked into the house. She and Rory had taken turns washing up in their shared bathroom before appearing for dinner.

But couldn't Kendra and Quinn tell that she and Rory were giving off sparks? If they did, they gave no indication. Kendra didn't glance across the table and say *Damaris, you're glowing!* Quinn didn't remark on her extra perkiness.

Evidently, even though she was all fizzy inside, it didn't show. During a meal composed of leftover wedding fare, conversation centered on the foal's birth, whether Ryker and April were having good weather in San Francisco, and which chores would take priority now that life was back to normal.

"And we will never, and I mean *never* have another all-equestrian ceremony," Kendra said. "I don't care if Trevor and Bryce did think it was cool. Not doing it again."

"I'll drink to that." Quinn raised his beer glass.

"But what a spectacular way for me to be introduced to Wild Creek Ranch." Rory pushed aside his empty plate. "I'll never forget seein' all those horses and riders lined up, almost like they were in formation."

"They *were* in formation," Quinn said. "We assigned numbered positions. Only way we could dream of having it work out. What a logistical nightmare. Ryker owes me several beers and a flight in the Beechcraft."

"He promised to take me up, too," Rory said. "Guess I'll have to ask for a raincheck."

"Why?" Kendra glanced at him. "He'll be back on Sunday."

"I'm sorry to say I'll likely be gone by then."

Damaris glanced down at her plate as cold reality sent a chill through her. Under the table, Rory reached for her hand and gave it a squeeze.

"You will?" Quinn looked surprised, too. "I was there when you told Ryker and April goodbye. I could swear you said you'd probably still be around. Has something changed?"

"Aye." Rory kept the explanation of his guddle brief. When he was finished, he slipped his hand in Damaris's again.

"That's quite a story," Kendra said. "But I can't say I'm sorry it happened since you're here. I just hate that you have to leave so soon."

"At first I thought I'd have to leave tomorrow, but if my brother just needs my deposition to start the process, I can give him that in an online interview. I'll still book a flight out on Saturday, but it buys me more time here."

Quinn put his napkin beside his plate. "Couldn't the whole thing be handled online?"

"Maybe, but that wouldn't be fair to Aleck, me over here havin' a good time while he's cleanin' up my mess for free. And it makes sense that he'll have a stronger case if I show up in the flesh."

Quinn nodded. "I can see that. A man needs to face his accusers."

"Exactly. I thought leavin' would be the kind thing for the lady, but turns out she's no lady. And I've ended up looking cowardly, like I'm guilty of misleadin' her."

Kendra leaned back in her chair. "That must stick in your craw."

"Aye."

"Listen, if Aleck agrees to this, I have a laptop you can use instead of your phone. That would be easier."

"I'd surely appreciate that. Thank you."

"You're welcome. I mostly work on my desktop anyway. And since this will be a highly personal interview, I advise you not to do it in your room or anywhere in the house where you might be interrupted or overheard. You can use the cabin. It has internet, too."

"That's a great idea." Damaris had been meaning to go up there ever since she'd arrived. "You'd have complete privacy."

"I don't remember seein' a cabin."

"You might not have noticed it," Kendra said. "It's up the hill a ways and blends in with the trees. It was built by the original homesteaders."

Rory nodded. "Now you say that, I might've heard somethin' about it from Gran and Grandpa."

"It was Ian's and my home when my folks were alive, then a play area for the kids. Zane lived in it for a while. That's when we did most of the renovations and added internet capability. Ryker spent time in it when he came home from the service. Last year I let Quinn stay there while he repaired his Harley."

"Yeah, I fell in love with that cabin."

Kendra poked him. "You fell in love with me, doofus."

He gave her a slow grin. "I fell for you long before I ever set foot in that cabin. But staying in a place with so much history was a nice bonus."

"It sounds like exactly what I need," Rory said. "I don't know how many sessions Aleck will be wantin', though, even if he agrees to this. Will it be a problem, me tyin' up your laptop and the cabin?"

Kendra waved a hand in the air. "Don't worry about it. I don't need either one this week. I just hope your brother goes along with this."

"I'll find out at quarter-to-five in the mornin'."

"Which will come sooner than we think." Kendra stood. "I can't speak for the rest of you, but I'm ready to clean up the kitchen and pack it in. I have a busy week starting tomorrow."

"Me, too." Quinn got up, too. "I'm starting a new project."

"Oh, hey!" Rory pushed back his chair and stood. "I can't believe I didn't say this earlier. I saw

Mated for Life in the Guzzlin' Grizzly today when Damaris took me on a tour of Eagles Nest. Absolutely amazin'. Sent shivers down my spine."

"Thank you."

Rory began gathering dishes. "I'd love to see more of your work."

"Well, I have some prints for sale in the GG Country Store, and there's another large original in the lobby of Raptors Rise."

"We should go over there tomorrow." Damaris picked up the serving dishes and carried them into the kitchen. "You wanted to anyway."

"I do. That's another reason I can't leave yet. I haven't been inside Pie in the Sky, either, and I need more riding lessons."

"That's right." Kendra opened the dishwasher and began loading it. "You and Damaris went out today. How'd it go?"

"He did a spectacular job." Damaris gave Kendra her most earnest gaze. "He has an instinctive feel for it."

"He does?" Quinn's forehead wrinkled. "I didn't quite see that yesterday."

"Jetlag can really mess with a body," Rory said. "I'm much more focused today. And rested."

"That's good." Kendra switched on the dishwasher.

"In fact, I wouldn't mind takin' a walk to the barn so I can get one more look at that wee foal. Anyone want to come with me?"

Damaris made sure she didn't grin like an idiot. "I'm up for that."

"Sounds lovely," Kendra said, "but I'm in for the night."

"Me, too." Quinn ran water in the sink and squirted dish soap for a few hand washables.

Kendra tossed a dishtowel over her shoulder. Then she glanced at Rory. "Weren't you just down there when you brought Diablo and Jake back?"

"Aye. But since I'll only be here a few more days, I can't get too much of that bonnie foal."

"No, I suppose not." The gleam in Kendra's eyes could mean she was catching on.

"I'm gonna grab a sweatshirt." Damaris left the kitchen before she started laughing. Two minutes later she went out the door with Rory. "She's on to us."

"She'd be blind if she wasn't. I thought for sure she'd say something at dinner. I can't stop lookin' at you." He took her hand and laced his fingers through hers as they walked quickly through the cool night toward the barn.

"I can't stop smiling."

"Noticed that." He chuckled. "Love havin' that effect on you, lass. And here we are, already."

"That's what happens when you race walk."

"I was motivated. Let me get the door." Lifting the bar holding it shut, he slid it open. "After you."

She stepped inside the dim interior and tucked her glasses in her pocket as the door closed behind her. "I know we can't—oof!" She found herself in his arms, crushed against his broad chest and kissed with enough raw heat to set their clothes on fire.

<u>20</u>

Kissing was all Rory was after, but he'd become so addicted to Damaris's full lips that he wouldn't sleep tonight if he couldn't taste them once more before he went to bed. He might not sleep anyway with his room right next to hers.

His eagerness had knocked his hat to the floor. He left it there as he delved into the most luscious mouth he'd ever encountered. Cupping her bottom, he drew her close, nestling her against his aching tadger.

He'd brought nothing with him, though, on purpose. Just a few kisses, and then they'd go back. Holding her was enough for…oh, hey, now, here was a surprise. Warm hands caressed his bare chest. While he'd been kissing, she'd been unbuttoning.

Lifting his head, he gazed at her. Her face was in shadow. "Dinna expect that of ye."

"No?" She pushed his shirt open and pressed her mouth against his hot skin.

"Ahhh, lass. Ye turn me inside out."

"That's what I had in mind." She reached for his belt buckle.

He caught her hands. "I dinna bring anythin'."

"I didn't expect you to. If you had we'd be gone far too long."

He tightened his grip on her hands. "And I only craved kissin' ye."

"I know, and I crave kissing you, too...someplace else. I've thought about it ever since the glen. It'll only take a minute. Then we'll go back."

"A *minute*?"

"Unless you resist me. Turn me loose so I can—"

"Nay." But he was weakening. "I dunna want ye to—"

"Are you sure?"

He dragged in a breath.

"Let me, Rory. Let me make love to your tadger."

He lost the fight with himself. The second he'd understood her plan, he'd desperately wanted her to go through with it. Trembling with anticipation, he slowly released her hands.

She let out a long sigh. "Good." She wasted no time getting to it, either. She quickly unbuckled, unzipped and dropped to her knees.

Then...praise be, he was transported to a world where warm fingers and an even warmer mouth were the only sensations that mattered. She wrapped him in pleasure so intense that he almost forgot the horses dozing nearby.

Just in time he stifled a groan, then gritted his teeth to hold back an even louder one as she increased the pressure and cupped his balls. That last bit did the trick. Fists clenched and head thrown back, he hissed through his teeth and let go. She milked him right proper, until his brain quit working and he feared he'd topple to the ground.

Gulping in air, he rested his hands on her shoulders to steady himself. "'Tis good. Verra good."

"I could tell." She gave him one last intimate kiss before tucking his happy tadger back inside his briefs. "You were shaking."

"Aye." Tightening his grasp on her shoulders, he pulled her to her feet. "Near fell over."

"You'll sleep well." She buttoned his shirt and cradled his face in her talented hands.

"Like a bairn."

Rising on her toes, she kissed him on the mouth.

Damned if the salty taste didn't stir his loins again. He drew her close. "I want a whole night with ye, lass. A night and the next mornin', so I can wake with ye in my arms."

"I'd love that." She caressed the bristle on his chin. Then she pulled her glasses out of her sweatshirt pocket and put them on.

He sucked in another steadying breath. "So that's where they went. Wondered if I'd knocked 'em off."

"I knew you'd want to kiss me so I put them away after we came in."

"And you'd already planned on that other?"

"If you'd let me."

"Tried to refuse."

"I'm glad you gave in." She smoothed the front of his shirt with her palm. "Let's go peek in on the foal."

"All right." He'd completely lost track of why they were here. Damaris took up every single brain cell he possessed. He'd not been this addlepated about a woman since his first crush at fifteen.

After dusting off his hat and putting it on, he followed her to the stall where Licorice and Eclipse were hidden in the shadows.

She glanced in and turned back to him with a smile. "Not much to see without the overhead lights."

He returned her smile. "Didn't expect there would be. Let's go."

After they left the barn, he recaptured her hand. The night breeze ruffled her hair, bringing the scent of it his way. "If we could have a whole night, I'd spend part of it brushin' your hair."

"You would?"

"Brushin' it, sifting it through my fingers, watchin' how the light plays on it."

"That sounds nice."

"It would be. I just wish..." He sighed. No point in talking about what he wished. In the distance an owl hooted. Then another answered. "Did you hear that?"

"The owls? I love listening to them. This is the time of year you hear them more often. They're pairing up."

"It's the same at home. There they go again." He climbed the porch steps, reluctant to go inside. "If I didn't have to get up so early, I'd sit out on the porch and listen to them. But I need to be alert for that call."

"Yes, you sure do."

He opened the door and waited for her to go in ahead of him. The house was quiet. Only one lamp was on in the living room. "Should we turn that off?"

"Yes. I'm sure they left it for us." Damaris switched it off and continued down the hallway.

He paused at her door and lowered his voice. "I'm goin' to think positive, that Aleck will go for this idea. If he does, he'll likely want to have our first video chat sometime after he gets off work at five. That's mid-mornin' here. That may be as far as I can plan until I talk with him."

"I know."

"When Kendra mentioned that cabin, were you thinkin' the same thing I was?"

"Probably."

"I won't sneak around, though."

"I don't want to, either. That would feel icky." She took a quick breath. "Let's take this one day at a time."

"Good advice." Leaning down, he gave her a slow, sweet kiss. "Goodnight, lass. You can have the lavy first."

"Okay." She gave him one more quick kiss. "See you in the morning."

"See you in my dreams." He winked at her and walked the short distance to his room. Guaranteed he'd dream about her all night. And wish like hell she could be sharing his bed.

* * *

The tune on Rory's cell chimed five minutes before he had to make his call. He cursed the chime for interrupting a most excellent time making love with Damaris. Not surprising that he had a woody as he climbed out of bed and shut off the alarm.

Stumbling to the bathroom in his underwear, he splashed cold water on his face. Considered splashing it on his woody but now that the dream was fading, it was going down of its own accord.

Back in his bedroom, he closed the door and picked up the phone. Then he took several deep breaths before tapping the screen and putting the phone to his ear.

"You're prompt. I'll give you that."

"Good mornin'."

"Afternoon, now, by one minute. Have you sorted things out on your end?"

This'll only take a minute. He smiled. He'd been so insulted by that...

"Rory? You there?"

"Sorry." He scrubbed a hand over his face. "Not quite awake yet."

"I know it's early, but we need to get this settled."

"Aye. Here's what I propose. As I understand it, you need my description of the events leading up to my night with Catriona."

"Correct. You'll tell it as you remember, but I'll be there to ask questions in case I need more clarification."

"Could we do it as a video chat?"

Aleck paused for a beat. "That's creative, but you still need to come home and show your face."

"But maybe not for a few days if you have that video to work from. Or more, if you need them. I can borrow Kendra's laptop."

"It's the woman, isn't it?"

"Her name's Damaris and yes, she's part of the reason. She's incredible. I love bein' with her. We just...get along."

"Could this go anywhere, though? Isn't she some university professor or somethin'?"

"She is and I don't know if this is goin' anywhere. But she's here, now, and I don't want to miss a single day with her if I can help it."

"Whoa, Rory. I haven't ever heard that kind of talk from you. Sounds serious."

"It could be serious. We only have this week, but she plans to visit Eagles Nest again and—"

"Would she move to Scotland?"

"I can't see her doin' that." But maybe Eagles Nest. "Right now she wants to stay with her think tank in California. She's doin' the kind of research that could get her a Nobel Prize."

"Wow."

"What about the video chat? Can we do that instead so I don't have to rush back? She leaves on Saturday for California. I can be home this weekend."

"Yeah, we can try it. Although seems to me the longer you're with her, the tougher it'll be to say goodbye."

"Sayin' goodbye will be tough no matter when I do it. I'm willin' to put up with that in return for these few days of bein' with her."

"If that's your choice, we can try to make it work."

"That's decent of you, Aleck."

"I'm just sorry that a woman you're crazy about may be lost to you. We have universities over here, too."

"I wouldn't ask that of her. If she moved anywhere, it would be back to Montana. She loves this ranch. Matter of fact, so do I."

"How's the cowboy thing comin' along?"

"I'm not much of a rider, yet, but I think I could be, given time. It appeals to me. Everythin' about the place does. After breakfast, I'm goin' to muck out some stalls."

"If that's what it sounds like, better you than me."

"Yeah, you'd probably hate it. So, this video chat, can we set it for after you get off work?"

"That's doable. I'll email you the instructions for connectin' on Kendra's laptop. Let's say five-thirty my time."

"Ten-thirty mine. I'll be there. Thanks, Aleck. This means a lot."

"I can tell. Hey, take some pictures on your phone and send them to me."

"Will do. I'll make sure to get you a good one of what I shovel today."

"You would, too. Later." Aleck was laughing as he disconnected.

Laughing was good. Empathy was good. Aleck wanted the best for him, a happy life.

He wanted that, too, and his path used to be clear. He'd land a well-paying job with a major distillery, fall in love with a bonnie Scottish lass who loved him back, and someday they'd have a couple of wee bairns. Now, the future was muddy, especially if Damaris wasn't in it.

21

Damaris backed away from the wall and rubbed the ear she'd pressed against it during Rory's conversation with his brother. He thought she was *incredible*? He didn't want to miss a *single day* with her?

She passed a mirror mounted above the dresser and stared into it in disbelief. She'd never inspired that kind of devotion in any man other than her father. Her dad had used the word incredible as in *my incredibly intelligent daughter.*

That wasn't the same as being called simply *incredible*, without any reference to her brainpower. The way Rory had said it seemed to encompass all of her—the whole person.

She wasn't positive what he'd meant when he'd said *I can't see her doin' that*, but likely it was a move to Scotland. Heaven help her, she might consider it if he asked, but it wouldn't be in her best interests.

He came out of his room, walked across the hall and closed the bathroom door. The shower came on. Voices filtered out from the master bedroom. Kendra and Quinn were up, too.

She peered out her door and theirs was still closed. Moving fast, she grabbed her bathrobe and scurried into Rory's room. She put on her robe and sat on his unmade bunk bed.

The rumpled covers carried the scent of his aftershave and she fought the urge to burrow under the sheets. Instead she got up and made his bed. It was the least she could do for a man who didn't want to miss a single day of being with her.

That blew her away. She wouldn't know if she hadn't eavesdropped. She should probably confess that she'd invaded his privacy. They'd been honest with each other from the beginning and she wasn't about to change that dynamic.

He took longer in the shower than she'd anticipated. Maybe he was shaving while he was in there. Some men did that. She couldn't claim to know his habits.

At last he walked into the room wearing only a towel. Glory be, the man was gorgeous. A few drops of water still clung to his chest hair.

The drops quivered when he gasped in surprise. "Damaris!" He nudged the door shut with his foot. "I didn't know you were up."

"My eyes popped open when I heard you go into the bathroom."

"Just now?"

"No, when you first went in there. I'm not proud of this, but I knew you had to call Aleck and I...listened at the wall."

His soft chuckle turned into a belly laugh.

"Shh! I don't want Kendra and Quinn to find me in here!"

"Wouldn't matter. You're wearin' your pajamas and your equations dressin' gown while perched on a neatly made bed. Not exactly a picture of debauchery."

"I've never been very good at debauchery."

"Except when you're in the barn at night with me."

"That wasn't—"

"I know, lass. I couldn't resist teasin' you. So you heard my conversation with Aleck? Then you must know he agreed to the video chat."

"I do, and that's great."

"Isn't it? I shouldn't have to go back until you leave. We'll have time to—"

"I also heard what you said about me."

"What did I...oh, right. I did talk a bit about you." His gaze became more focused. "And?"

"You told him I was incredible."

His voice softened. "Which you are. That's why I—"

"Want to spend every single day with me?"

He took a deep breath. "I did say that and it's the God's truth. I know we may not have a solid future, but I'm greedy for whatever we can have."

"Did he ask if I'd be willing to move to Scotland?"

"Yes, and I told him that wouldn't work."

"Rory, if we mean this much to each other, then—"

"It's because you mean so much to me that I wouldn't want you to consider it. Maybe you'd find kindred spirits and maybe you wouldn't. It's not worth the risk."

"But—"

"I mean it, Damaris. I'm sure you had your pick of universities and you chose Caltech for a reason. I'll not be the bloke who derailed a promisin' career. I'll not have that on my conscience."

"But what about us?"

He came over and sat beside her on the bed, bringing his freshly shaved and washed aroma with him. "All right, full disclosure." He met her gaze. "If I could absolutely guarantee that a life with me wouldn't harm your chances of a breakthrough on your research or sabotage your likelihood of winnin' that prize, I'd want to have that conversation with ye." Sadness turned his blue eyes to gray. "But I canna guarantee that, Damaris."

She touched his arm. "Your brogue peeked out just now. You're not drunk. Are you—"

"Nay." He stared at his clenched hands. "I'm...emotional. Dunna want to think of leavin' ye. That's the other time I slip." He swallowed. "But a man dunna share that with just anyone."

"I'm honored you shared it with me."

"I feel like I can share anythin' with ye." He glanced at her. "You're the same with me. Ye canna eavesdrop without tellin' me. I love that you had to come in here and confess."

"Eavesdropping is wrong."

"Not when the conversation matters to ye. I would have done the same."

"That helps."

A knock came at the door. "Rory? You up? I thought I heard the shower."

"I'm up, Aunt Kendra! Be right out."

"Good. I want to hear what your brother had to say. Coffee's made."

"Thanks. Be right there." He took a deep breath and cleared his throat. When he turned, his eyes shone with purpose. "Fair warnin', lass. I'm goin' to ask Kendra if I can move into the cabin."

She blinked. "Just like that?"

"Just like that."

"Bold move."

"I think she respects bold moves. They seem to run in the family."

"And you are a McGavin."

"Aye."

"I'm going to take the fastest shower in history." She stood. "Can you hold off asking her until I'm in there?"

"Sure thing."

* * *

Their places were set at the dining table again instead of at the smaller kitchen table. Damaris took it as a signal that Kendra knew this breakfast discussion would be important.

Rory came out of the kitchen and placed a thermal coffee carafe on the table. He flashed Damaris a smile, then called to Kendra. "Damaris is here."

"Good! Eggs are about ready."

"What can I do to help?"

"Not a thing," Quinn said as he set out coffee mugs. "Have a seat."

She took the one she'd had the night before.

"Here we go." Kendra brought out a bowl of fluffy scrambled eggs and another of country fries. She set them in the middle of the table. "Pour yourself some coffee and dish yourself eggs and potatoes. Bacon and a fruit bowl are on the way."

"Fruit bowl has arrived." Quinn set it down with a flourish.

"And bacon." Rory brought in a platter of bacon strips that had been perfectly browned. After setting it on the table, he took his seat next to her.

"Terrific service at this restaurant." She poured herself coffee and passed it over to him.

Quinn chuckled. "Our staff is well trained."

"That's the truth." Kendra smiled at Quinn as he held her chair. "Dish up quick everybody. I can't wait to hear Rory's news."

"Me, either." Damaris almost forgot to say it.

"Although I'm guessing it's good news," Kendra added, "since he's been smiling ever since he came out of his room."

"It is good news," Rory said as soon as everyone had food. "Aleck will send me instructions for signin' into the platform he uses. I'll connect with him at ten-thirty this mornin'."

"Fabulous." Kendra beamed at him. "So we'll have you until Saturday."

"Glad to hear it, son," Quinn said. "Wish you could hang around longer, but I understand that this needs to be handled."

"I'll get my laptop as soon as we finish eating," Kendra said. "And I'll take you up to the cabin. It might need a dust cloth here and there, but everything's turned on—heat, water. There's a little kitchen table you can use for the laptop."

"Should work great. I appreciate the use of both things. You've been more than generous to a bloke who showed up uninvited on your doorstep."

"You're family, Rory. I'm so glad you came to visit."

"It's been special for me, too, in many ways." He took a deep breath. "And because of that, I have one more request."

"Which is?"

"I'm askin' your permission to move into the cabin for the rest of my stay."

Kendra looked startled but she recovered quickly. "Why, sure, I don't see why not. It's a charming place, and—"

"There's more. I'd like to invite Damaris to stay with me."

22

Kendra's mouth dropped open. For one heart-pounding moment, Rory was afraid she would refuse.

Instead she began to laugh. "Oh, my God. I was right on the timing." She turned to Quinn. "I win. Pay up."

Quinn reached in his back pocket for his wallet and pulled out a twenty. "Clearly your nephew is a gutsier man than I am." He held out the bill to Kendra.

She plucked it from his fingers and shoved it in the pocket of her jeans. "Thanks for coming through for me, Rory. I always knew you had the McGavin cojones and this proves it."

At a loss for words, Rory stared at her.

Quinn picked up his coffee mug and raised it in salute. "I have to hand it to you, son. I didn't think you'd get up the nerve to make that request for another couple of days."

"You two were *expectin'* me to ask this?"

"Oh, yeah." Kendra helped herself to more fruit. "We've seen the way you and Damaris look at each other, yet both of you are too well-bred to carry on when we're right down the hall. I even wondered if Damaris would get me aside and ask about the cabin."

"I didn't think of it." Damaris's cheeks were pink. "And even if I had, I doubt I'd have screwed up the courage to broach the subject."

"Good thing you have your knight in shining armor, here. All I had to do was let him know there was a cabin on the property and he took it from there."

"Speaking of that." Quinn rolled his eyes. "I shot myself in the foot by raving about how much I love that cabin. If I'd kept my mouth shut, maybe Rory wouldn't have come up with this plan so fast and I'd be twenty bucks richer."

"Wait a minute." Rory looked at Kendra. "You suggested usin' the cabin as a quiet place to do the video chat, which has nothin' to do with—"

"You could have staged a video chat in your bedroom, no problem. Last week we had people running in and out of here, but this week?" She shrugged. "You'd have all the privacy in the world."

"I'll be damned."

"I do have one request of you, though."

"Anythin'."

"Please don't lock yourselves away up there for the duration. I like you both very much and so does the rest of the extended family. We want to see you now and then this week."

"Oh, we would never hide away up there," Damaris said. "That would be rude."

But tempting. Rory nodded in agreement, though. "No hidin'. I want to get better acquainted with everyone, and see more of this wee town, and—"

"Take more horseback rides and polish your skills?" Kendra arched a brow.

"Yes!" Damaris turned to him. "Now we can actually go riding for real instead of..." She stopped and her eyes widened behind her glasses. Her cheeks had been pink before, but now they were bright red. "I mean...um...oh, Lord." She covered her face with her hands.

"Never you mind, lass." He gently drew her hands away and gave her a smile. "They've been on to us all along. It's just out in the open, now. Which is better."

"Much better," Kendra said. "I've been waiting for the other shoe to drop."

"My ma says that all the time."

"Yep. That's a mother's job, all right—monitoring the other shoe."

Damaris cleared her throat and took a breath. "Well, you sure called this one. Now I have to ask. Was the whole family in on the bet?"

"Goodness, no. This was a friendly wager between Quinn and me. I haven't discussed this with anybody else."

"Not even Mandy?"

"Nope. I won't announce this move to the cabin, but some family members might notice and ask about it. What do you want me to say?"

"Tell you what," Damaris said. "I'll give Mandy a call and tell her."

Kendra nodded. "Good idea."

"Then I'll give her carte blanche to inform anybody she thinks might care. That way when I have coffee with everyone on Wednesday, the word will be out."

"Excellent. If that's settled, we should get a move on. Quinn, have you heard from Jim this morning?"

Quinn pulled his phone from his pocket and checked the screen. "He just arrived at the barn. Says the little guy's doing well. I'd like to go down there, though, see for myself. Then I'm off to my studio."

"See you at lunch."

"You bet." He gave her a quick kiss and headed for the door.

She turned to Rory and Damaris. "I'll take care of cleanup so you can pack your stuff."

"That would be great." He walked around the table and gave her a hug. "Thank you."

"Yes, thank you." Damaris hugged her, too.

"You're both very welcome. I'll meet you by the front door in ten minutes."

Rory followed Damaris through the living room and down the hall. "Won't take me long. I never completely unpacked."

"Won't take me long because I'll just throw everything in there and straighten it out later." When she reached his door, she whirled around, grabbed his face in both hands and planted one on him, bumping his nose in the process. She drew back, laughing. "You *did it.*"

"Aye." He was damned proud of himself, too.

"I'm so excited I could bust. Is it true that you brought a kilt and your plaid?"

"It's true." His eyes sparkled. "Would you be wantin' me to model it for you tonight?"

"You read my mind."

"I tucked it in my suitcase for the hell of it. Then I got here and wondered why I had. It wasn't like I was goin' to put it on and do the Highland Fling."

"You brought it so I could see you wearing it."

"Aye." He grinned. "In the traditional way."

"Whew!" She fanned herself. "I'm getting out of here before I back you up against the wall and ravish you."

"Save that thought for later."

"I will. See you in…seven minutes." She dashed into her bedroom.

He made it to the living room before she did, but she arrived shortly after with a bulging suitcase, a backpack and a duffel.

She glanced at his sleek suitcase, half the size of hers and laughed. "I'm outclassed."

"Aleck loaned me his. He's the international traveler, not me. This holds more than it looks like."

"Let me lift yours." She picked it up. "As I thought. Light as a feather. While mine—"

"You won't be carryin' it." He hoisted her suitcase and duffel in one hand and his suitcase in the other.

"I'm swooning right here. Just so you know."

"Good." He smiled. "That'll come in handy later."

"Ready, kids?" Kendra came out of the kitchen with a spray bottle, a dust rag, and a bag of what looked like linens. "Hey, Rory, that's impressive."

"He wrestles barrels of whiskey back home."

"Clearly he wins that contest every time. Let's go." She went out the door.

Damaris grabbed her backpack, pressed her hand to her heart and batted her eyes before following Kendra.

He was still laughing as he brought up the rear on the way to the cabin. She was irrepressible, his Damaris. *His Damaris.* Not exactly accurate, was it, now? But maybe it could be.

The log cabin was easy to see now that he knew it was there. No telling how he'd missed it before. Must have been too involved with the wedding, Damaris, the foaling, Damaris...

If he'd been able to design the perfect Western setting for a cozy rendezvous, he couldn't top this. Early morning sunlight dappled the porch and two wooden chairs with slanted seats and backs. Adirondacks? Maybe. A stone chimney rose above a galvanized tin roof.

The sky was clear, but if he could be lucky enough to have a little rain tonight on that roof, combined with a cheerful fire and Damaris, life didn't get much better. But all he truly needed out of that grouping was Damaris.

The inside was even more inviting, since a bed covered in a colorful quilt was the dominant piece of furniture in the open concept interior. A battered easy chair sat in front of the fireplace. He and Damaris could probably share it. A tight fit would be fine with him.

Kendra set down the linens, spray bottle and dusting rag. "I'm gonna open the windows to air it out. You can close them later if you get chilly."

"This place is right out of the movies I used to watch as a kid." Rory put the suitcases next to the bed. "Only those were movie sets and this is real."

"Sometimes after a riding lesson Kendra would let me come up here and read on the porch. I pretended I was a pioneer woman."

Kendra chuckled. "When Ian and I lived here I *was* a pioneer woman. That kitchen is okay for a few days, but it has its limits." She picked up the spray bottle and the dust rag. "You two will be coming to the house to eat, right?"

"Yes, please," Damaris said. "I'm not a good cook under the best of circumstances."

"I am," Rory said, "but—"

"You can cook?" Damaris's eyes widened. "Kendra, is it just me, or is he the perfect guy?"

"He's close." She wiped off the small kitchen table and the counters. "Then again, I'm prejudiced in favor of a certain Sawyer dude. Who also can cook." She glanced around. "So, you have linens and there's enough firewood for tonight. We can replenish it in the morning. I'll leave you two to settle in."

"I'm not settlin' in quite yet." Rory looked over at Damaris. "There's a wheelbarrow and a shovel down at the barn callin' my name."

She gave a quick nod. "Same here."

"You're gonna muck out stalls?" Kendra clearly thought they were nuts. "When I asked you to be a part of things, I didn't mean shoveling horse apples."

"Horse apples? You lost me."

"Euphemism for horse poop. I appreciate the impulse, but why not stay here and settle in? Prepare for your ten-thirty video chat."

"I can't think of anythin' better to prepare me than shovelin' horse apples."

"Well, I sure can, but it's your call."

"Besides, I promised Aleck a picture of a wheelbarrow full of them."

She stared at him. "Really?"

"Really."

"You Scots are strange. Okay, then, I'll walk with you and check on Licorice and Eclipse."

"I always liked mucking out stalls," Damaris said as they headed back down the hill. "I used to figure out my physics homework while I shoveled and raked."

"I do sort of remember that. Are you hoping it might give you a breakthrough on your research project?"

"Nah. I just want to watch Rory get all hot and sweaty." She winked at him.

Kendra laughed. "Now that I understand."

23

Watching Rory shovel turned out to be as exciting as Damaris had anticipated, especially when he took off his shirt and used it to wipe his face. Cody had given him some basic instruction before leaving Damaris to supervise.

They'd been working alone for quite a while, chatting now and then. Casual though it all seemed, she'd worked herself into a sensual lather. If Rory hadn't been locked into the video chat at ten-thirty, she would have suggested having fun getting cleaned up together.

But he did have the chat and she didn't plan to be there. She finally told him so while they sat on a straw bale during a break from their labors in the barn. He'd put his shirt back on, but just her luck he hadn't buttoned it.

He took off his hat and ran his fingers through his sweat-dampened hair. "I don't expect you to be sittin' where Aleck can see you." He put down his hat. "I wouldn't try to introduce you or anythin'."

"Good, because that would be extremely awkward." Tantalizing glimpses of his bare chest through the opening in his shirt gave her heart palpitations.

He seemed oblivious. "I can see why you wouldn't want to be in range of the lens, but you can sit nearby. And give me moral support."

"Do you need me there? Because if that's the case, I'll reconsider."

He gazed at her. "Nay, I don't *need* you there, although it would be nice. But since I'm in the right on this, I'm not nervous about it. Honestly, it'll be a relief to share the details with Aleck."

"That's why I'd rather not be there. I don't want to hear the details of how Catriona schemed to get you into her bed and then turned on you when you refused to become her lap dog. I'd just want to fly over there and pull her hair out by the roots. That's not a good idea for many reasons."

"You'd go over and pull her hair out?" He seemed tickled by that concept. "Have you ever had a physical fight with someone?"

"No, just the verbal kind, but there's always a first time for everything. I get furious just thinking about what she did without knowing the details. Once I know them I might lose it."

"Lose it? You?"

"It could happen. Let's not take that chance."

"I'm fascinated by the concept of you losin' it."

"You've already seen me do it, just in a different context."

"I have?" When he shifted his weight on the hay bale, his shirt moved enough to reveal the red-gold of his chest hair caressed by sunlight.

She curled her fingers into her palms. Then she lowered her voice, even though no one was there to hear except Licorice and Eclipse, the only horses still in the barn. "When I come."

"Oh. But you're not angry, then."

"No, but I'm not filtering my response, either. That's how I define losing it." Which she might any time, now. She could almost taste the sweat on his skin.

"I'm glad you clarified." He smiled. "I'm lookin' forward to the next time you lose it."

"Believe me, so am I." Unless it turned out to be now, which would demonstrate how little self-control she had. "But after what Kendra said, I want to hold off on our disappearing act until after dinner."

"I wish we didn't have to wait so long, but I'm with you on that. I decided the same thing. Daylight is for bein' with friends and family. Nighttime is for..." He reached up and stroked her cheek with one finger. "Losin' it."

She gulped. "Rory McGavin, you're too hot for your own good. I'm about ready to change the plan and spend the whole afternoon in bed with your sexy self."

"You are? Then let's do it. We'll worry about friends and family tomorrow."

"No, let's not. It sets a bad precedent. We talked about going over to Zane's raptor center today. If we don't start checking things off the list, we'll get to Saturday and you won't have done everything you wanted."

"Except make love to you. That's at the top of my list."

"We can do that at night. We have the cabin, now, which neither of us anticipated yesterday. Our opportunities for making love just expanded exponentially."

"Say that last part again."

"Why? Didn't you get what I meant?"

"Oh, I did, lass. I just love hearing how you phrase things."

God, his eyes were blue. She was in real danger of falling into a sensual haze. That could lead to bad judgment and a disregard of Kendra's simple request. "We need to create a schedule."

His eyes sparkled. "On a spreadsheet?"

"Hey, don't tease. You loved my spreadsheet."

"I did. I do. But speakin' of sheets..."

"Stop."

"Aye, I will. Start schedulin'."

"Let's tackle one day at a time. Here's a possibility for the rest of today. Text me when you're finished with your video chat. We'll head into town. I found out they serve lunch at Pie in the Sky now, so we can eat there. After that we'll go over to Raptors Rise. Sound good?"

"Sure."

"I've decided instead of calling Mandy this morning I'll go see her in person if she's available. While I'm there I'll pop over to Raptors Rise and let Zane know we're coming to the center, probably mid-afternoon."

"All right."

"One more thing. I'll bet you'll want to take another shower before that video chat so you'll look cool and collected."

"I guess that's a good idea, huh? I hadn't factored that in."

"It is a good idea, and I need to do the same before I go see Mandy." She consulted the time on her phone. "It's later than I thought. We're crunched on time if we each want to shower."

"We can take one together."

"No, we can't."

"Meaning we won't fit? I didn't check the size of the—"

"It's not a matter of fitting, although I doubt we would manage easily. It's a matter of getting naked together and expecting to go on about our business during and after."

"Mm. I see your point."

"The prudent solution is for me to shower now so I'll be off to Mandy's and out of your way when you're getting ready for the chat."

"Guess so. Then you're takin' off?"

"I'd better. We're almost done with the stalls." She stood.

"We are." He levered himself off the hay bale. "Go ahead. I'll finish up."

"Did you get your pictures for Aleck?"

"Not yet. Thanks for remindin' me."

"I'll see you later." She gave him a peck on the cheek because anything more might get her into trouble.

"Oh, no, you don't." He slipped his hand around her waist and pulled her close. "If I must wait for hours, I need a proper kiss."

She met his gaze and sucked in a breath. God, he was focused. Intense. She shivered. "When you look at me like that, you can have anything you want."

"Just a wee kiss." His voice rumbled softly in the silent barn. "Dunna want to ruin the schedule." His lashes fluttered down as he lowered his head, muting the effect of that laser-sharp gaze. Then his lips took over.

Gentle pressure gradually deepened to a no-holds-barred assault that was new, different. Her surroundings faded. There was only Rory…

She moaned and clung to him, a willow in the wind of a passion that swept her into the teeth of the storm. And then, with exquisite tenderness, he brought her back to earth.

Lifting his head, he slowly released her and stepped back. "Thank ye, lass."

She nodded, not trusting herself to form words, let alone a complete sentence. Lifting a hand in farewell, she turned and left the barn. If she concentrated, she might be able to walk without tripping. What had he put in that kiss, anyway?

The effects of it lingered as she showered in a bathroom the size of one she'd had in a low-budget stateroom during a weekend cruise to Mexico in her undergraduate days. She and Rory wouldn't fit in here together, let alone manage to have sexy times.

It would be funny to try, though. They'd get a laugh out of it and move the party elsewhere. Ah, Rory...the hot water turned cold before she came to her senses and shut it off.

She dressed quickly and called Mandy, who sounded excited to see her. Maybe Zane had mentioned the horseback ride yesterday. Mandy would have put a whole different spin on it than Zane.

Mandy now lived in her childhood home, which she and Zane had bought from her mother, so Damaris knew exactly how to get there. Taking her phone, she set out along the wooded path that connected Wild Creek Ranch property to the acreage that now included Raptors Rise.

Walking over to Mandy's was a treat. The small scale of Eagles Nest stood in sharp contrast to Pasadena and neighboring LA. She rode a bus to Caltech, which was an improvement over driving the freeway, but she wouldn't say it was a relaxing trip. She and relaxation hadn't spent much time together since she'd left Eagles Nest, but the college atmosphere was stimulating.

Mandy flung open the front door. "I've been pacing the floor waiting for you." She tucked her blond hair behind her ears. "And when you're lugging a kid around inside you, pacing is a chore."

"Why were you pacing?"

"Zane said you guys went riding yesterday and now you asked to come over, so naturally I figured something's happened! Am I right?"

"Well, I—"

"Wait, wait. I'm being a terrible hostess. I've made coffee. Come in. I should at least let you sit before I grill you. I have chocolate chip cookies." She swept a hand toward a familiar dining table by a large picture window. A platter of cookies took center stage.

"Aw, you still have that table. I used to love eating snacks there."

"Mom said it belongs by the window so she left it. She made the cookies, too. She's gonna be an awesome grandma. So, coffee?"

"Love some."

"It's decaf because that's all I drink these days, but if you want regular I'll make that."

"Decaf's fine."

"Be right back." She hurried into the kitchen.

"You don't have to wait on me. I'll come get it." She walked into the kitchen. "The place looks great."

"We've done some painting. Before you leave I'll show you the baby's room."

"You can show me now, if you want."

"Are you kidding? I'm dying to hear what's going on with that hot Scot."

Damaris snorted.

"Well, he is." She handed over a mug of coffee. "Do you take anything in it?"

"Just black."

"Here you go." She made a shooing motion. "Go sit. Tell me everything."

"Um..."

Mandy's eyes widened. "Oh, my God, you two *did it*! On the ride?"

"Yeah." She started grinning and almost giggled. She was *not* a giggler.

"Was it awesome? Never mind. All I have to do is look at you to know it was spectacular. Put down your coffee. I want to give you a hug."

She set her coffee on the table.

"I'm so happy for you." Mandy gave her a bear hug. "What happens now?"

"This morning he asked Kendra if both of us could move into the cabin for the rest of our stay and she said we could."

"Woot! What a guy!" Then she paused. "Why are you here with me instead of over there making whoopee?"

"It's complicated." She chose a seat facing the view of the woods.

Mandy sat catty-corner from her. "I hope you didn't have a fight already."

"No fight. It really is complicated, but I'll try to keep it brief."

"Drag it out all you want. Gives me an excuse to eat cookies."

They'd put quite a dent in the pile by the time Damaris finished describing Rory's issue and his brother's attempt to repair the damage.

"Please don't tell me this is one of those tear-jerker love stories with a sucky ending."

She took a deep breath. "It's not, but neither of us have the answer."

"Move to Scotland. You'll be fine over there."

"You know, I might be, but if I don't find a good academic fit, that would be bad. Caltech is perfect for me."

"Then maybe he needs to come over here."

"He's excited about making Scotch and Scotland's the place to do it. Besides, he'd be leaving his family."

"I know, but—"

"If Rory and I are going to be together, it needs to be win-win, each of us doing what we're meant to do, without painful sacrifices we might regret later."

"That's sounds very evolved and noble, but the way you describe the situation, I don't see a solution."

"That doesn't mean there isn't one. I can't believe we'd meet, make this special connection, and then be unable to work it out."

"You're both certainly smart enough, especially you."

"This isn't about using our heads." She gazed at Mandy. "It's about using our hearts."

24

Despite what Rory had told Damaris, he was drained by the end of the interview. Aleck thought it might be enough, thank God. He didn't want to talk about it anymore.

He texted Damaris and discovered she was walking back from Mandy and Zane's. She described how to find the beginning of the woodland path and he headed out. Ah. Sunshine on his back, a breeze making the pine branches sigh, birds in the trees and Damaris coming his way. Better, now.

When he glimpsed her through the trees, he lengthened his stride. She waved and started to run. He did, too, focusing on her smile. Almost tripped on a half-buried root because he wasn't watching where he was going.

When they met, it wasn't like in the movies, where a graceful slow-motion sequence ended with him twirling her around. They smacked into each other and damned near fell. He couldn't kiss her because he was doubled over laughing. She was in the same fix.

Eventually he straightened and wiped the tears from his eyes. "That maneuver could use some work."

She took off her glasses and wiped her face on her sleeve. "It always looks so romantic in the movies, but maybe that was after a hundred takes."

"I'd believe it." He drew in a lungful of air scented with evergreen and the aroma of her shampoo. Their wee shower had smelled so much like her he'd almost developed a woody.

"How did it go with Aleck?"

"Fine. I think we might be done. I hope so."

She put on her glasses. "Want to talk about it?"

He shook his head.

"Okay." She held out her hand. "Ready to go have a great lunch at Pie in the Sky?"

"I'd tell you what I'm ready for, but since that's a non-starter, let's have lunch. I probably shouldn't even kiss you."

"If the last one you gave me is any example, you probably shouldn't. That was a doozy."

"Aye. Rocked me back, too. Took a few minutes before I was up to shovelin'." He laced his fingers through hers as they started back toward the ranch.

"Maybe we should ration ourselves until tonight."

"Sad to say, maybe we should." He might have communicated a wee bit too much with that kiss. Even if he hadn't come right out and said how he felt about her, she could have formulated an idea by now. Best not to discuss that, either.

"I texted Kendra to let her know our plans for the afternoon."

"Good."

"I offered to pick up dessert for tonight and she said Quinn's partial to cherry pie so we'll see if they have some."

"I hope they do. I'm partial to that myself." He wasn't kissing her as he'd longed to do, but just strolling along a sunny path holding hands and talking about ordinary things soothed his soul.

"Zane's looking forward to us coming by this afternoon. He asked how you liked mucking out stalls. I said you seemed happy enough when you were doing it."

"I was. I've never minded the work that comes with carin' for animals. It's satisfyin'. The company was good, too."

"Then you'd be willing to pitch in every morning?"

"Definitely.   I   appreciate   Kendra's hospitality so helpin' out seems like the thing to do."

"And it's the cowboy way."

"Oh, yeah?"

"Any good hand likes being useful. Besides, most of the ones I've known say mucking out stalls keeps them grounded."

"Makes sense." The more he learned about this life, the better he liked it.

"We're almost there. Do you need to go inside for anything?"

"Nope. Got the keys in my pocket. And just so you know, that's all I have in my pocket."

"That's as it should be." She walked along without saying anything for a while.

He didn't say anything, either. Likely they were both focused on the subject they weren't supposed to be focused on.

She broke the silence first. "What colors are in your plaid?"

"Where'd that question come from?"

"Just wondering."

Sure, she was. "Green, black, dark blue and white with a wee red stripe. My gran and grandpa researched it. May not be quite like the original, but it's close." He glanced at her. "Wouldn't be anticipatin' our evenin', would you, now?"

"Who, me?"

"Now you got me thinkin' about it." Like he hadn't been before. "And wantin' to be with ye."

She squeezed his hand. "We'll have our time together. I shouldn't have asked about your plaid. I just..."

"I understand, lass. It's not easy to put such matters out of your mind. We're navigatin' a tricky path, and I'm not talkin' about this one."

* * *

Pie in the Sky lived up to his expectations and then some. He didn't quite fit in the wee metal chairs, but once he tasted his thick sandwich made with homemade bread he didn't care whether those chairs were comfortable or not. By the time he bit into the best fudge brownie ever, he'd decided those chairs were fine.

One hunger satisfied, anyway. Next stop, Raptors Rise. He backed out of the parking space with more confidence than he'd had the day before. "Let's put this place on the schedule for tomorrow, too."

"Fine with me. I'm glad you liked it."

"I haven't found a single thing in this town I don't like."

"Yes, you have."

"Name it."

"Catsup."

He grinned. "I was puttin' on a show for you. I don't hate it all that much. I noticed they have hamburgers at the GG. I could probably tolerate catsup on one of those."

"We'll test it. We'll pick a night to go there for dinner."

"And dancin'?"

"I'd love that."

He glanced at her in surprise. "Truly?"

"I keep thinking about that waltz in Pills and Pop. Once I found the rhythm, it was like floating in your arms. I want to try it again."

"Then we will." Her eagerness to waltz with him made him ridiculously happy. "Maybe we should go tonight after dinner."

"It's a thought, except...I was hoping to have you all to myself."

"Oh." His groin tightened. "Right. Forget the GG. Don't know what I was thinkin'."

"We can go another night. We'll have four more to choose from."

"Aye." Five nights. Four full days. They'd go by like lightning. Saturday would be here before he could blink.

"Well, except Thursday. Mandy's hosting a girls' movie night and I said I'd go. But that still leaves three nights for the GG."

"Sure does." Without warning, several hours he'd been hoarding like a miser had just been snatched away. He'd take the hit like a man, though. He had no right to monopolize her, even if that was exactly what he—

"You missed the turn."

"No, I didn't. The ranch road is up ahead."

"I mean the turn for Raptors Rise."

"Why, so I did. Was wool gatherin' and lost track of the plan." He pulled to the shoulder, checked for traffic, and made a quick U-turn. "Let me know when it's comin' up."

"You didn't go very far past it. There it is. See the sign?"

"Yep." He put on his signal, waited for a couple of pickups to go by and turned in. "Wouldn't mind havin' one of those to drive."

"A truck?"

"Seems like the right thing for this area."

"When I got my license, I wanted one so bad. But I had no excuse for driving a truck. I didn't need to haul hay or pull a horse trailer." She leaned forward. "Around this curve the road forks. Go to the right and follow the signs to the visitor's center."

"It's nice this operation is tucked away in the woods."

"Zane was determined to create it that way for the sake of the birds. Some people advised him to rent a storefront in town and take some of the birds there for more visibility. He chose not to."

"Good man." He found a parking space. "Plenty of cars."

"Word is spreading." She started to open her door and paused. "Remember the Sawyer grouping on my spreadsheet?"

"It's vague in my mind, lass. I have a bead on Quinn, Roxanne, and Wes. After that it's chaos."

"You're only missing two—Pete, the oldest, and Gage, the middle son. I only bring it up because Gage works here. I had a chance to talk with him at the rehearsal dinner. He walked into this facility last year and fell in love with it. You might do the same."

He gazed at her. "I likely will, but why do you think so?"

"You almost went into wildlife management. I understand why you didn't chose it, but this operation isn't about managing wild creatures. It's about saving them."

He nodded. "That speaks to me." He opened his door. "I'm eager to meet Gage."

The middle Sawyer son wasn't difficult to find. Damaris pointed him out the minute they stepped into the spacious lobby. His bearing and the tilt of his Stetson marked him as Quinn's son, but his dark hair must have come from his mother. He stood inside a semi-circle of visitors with a golden eagle perched on his arm.

A leather gauntlet protected him from the bird's talons. A healthy, mature golden had a grip powerful enough to carry off a newborn lamb. Rory had seen it happen.

Behind Gage, Quinn's impressive artwork depicted a bald eagle family in a massive nest—mother, father and three fledglings. A plaque next to it read *Home Sweet Home.* Rory beckoned to Damaris and they joined the group.

They'd missed part of the presentation, but Rory got the gist. The eagle had been shot several times and left for dead. Four operations later, she was mostly healed but would never fly again.

"We've named her Victory," Gage said, "and she's become the face of Raptors Rise. We're determined to win this fight to protect our magnificent birds of prey. Thank you for your attention and your support."

Rory applauded with the rest of the group, his heart full as he met the solemn gaze of that noble bird. Then he glanced at Damaris. "Thank you for makin' sure we came here."

She smiled up at him, her green eyes luminous. "In love, yet?"

A sucker punch to the gut. He gulped for air. Only one answer to that question. "Aye."

25

Damaris stared at Rory in dismay. "I didn't mean…"

"Are ye sure?" His voice was soft, the light in his eyes tender.

She met his warm gaze and took a shaky breath. "No."

"Dinna think so." His smile held a tinge of sorrow.

She swallowed. "Me, too, Rory."

He nodded. "I know, lass."

"Hey, Damaris." She turned as Gage came toward them, the golden eagle on his arm. "Zane said you two were coming by. Rory, I don't think we've officially met. I'm Gage Sawyer."

"Glad to know you." Rory extended his hand. "Never been this close to a golden. She doesn't seem nervous bein' around so many people."

"Victory's been our ambassador for a while. We eased her into it gradually and now she takes it all in stride. If you two would like to come with me, I'll carry her back to her enclosure. Then I'll text Zane and see if he's free. If not, I'd be happy to take you around."

"Thanks, Gage." The brief discussion about Victory had allowed Damaris to calm herself after her Freudian slip. "I've heard so much about this place that I feel as if I've already toured it, but I haven't."

"Then you're in for a treat. Follow me." He started down a hallway. Victory swiveled her head to watch Damaris and Rory as they walked behind him.

"She's keeping an eye on us," Damaris said.

"Aye." He gave her shoulder a quick squeeze and lowered his voice. "It'll be all right, lass."

"I know it will." Somehow.

The tour of Raptors Rise provided a strong dose of optimism. Zane had created something beautiful and hopeful with his rescue operation. Eagles, hawks, falcons and owls had roomy enclosures tucked into the trees. Most were slated to be released once their medical problems had been resolved. Victory's story was the exception, not the rule.

The nursery was a revelation, too. Badger's name was on it because he'd donated a chunk of money from his sizable trust fund to equip the room. Rory couldn't stop talking about that nursery as they drove back to Wild Creek.

"Those wee birds, Damaris! Nothin' but piles of fluff. And without Raptors Rise, they wouldn't make it. I wish I'd known durin' the weddin' that Badger gave the money for that nursery. I'd like to shake his hand."

"Why don't I find out what his schedule is like this week? Ryker won't be back to take you up in the Beechcraft, but Badger would probably get a kick out of showing you Eagles Nest from the air."

"Would you come with me?"

"Sure. Do small planes make you nervous?"

He smiled. "Nay. Love 'em. Just want to be with you as much as I can."

Her heart turned over. "Ditto."

* * *

They made it back in time to help feed the horses and spend a few minutes watching Eclipse learning how to walk on his spindly legs. Dinner was only the four of them again.

The prospect of going back to the cabin after the meal tempted Damaris to bolt her food, but a lively discussion about the visit to Raptors Rise kept her from eating too fast. Good thing. Indigestion wasn't romantic.

Rory seemed to be pacing himself, too, until pie and coffee were served. He'd polished off his slice before she was half-finished with hers.

"Goodness, you must like cherry pie," Kendra said. "How about another piece?"

"I do love it, but no more for me, thank you." He took a sip of his coffee and settled back in his chair. "How did Zane get started rescuin' birds of prey?"

"He's always loved raptors," Kendra said. "He was living up in the cabin when he brought home his first injured golden. Built an enclosure for it near the cabin, nursed it back to health and released it again. That was the beginning."

"Amazin'." Rory drummed his fingers silently against his thigh. "He just did what came naturally. I admire that enterprisin' spirit."

"Me, too," Damaris said. "I didn't know that's how he started." She ate faster as Rory asked more questions about the growth of the operation. Meanwhile his fingers continued their restless tapping.

Damaris finished her pie, but Kendra and Quinn were still eating theirs. She picked up her coffee mug and took a sip while moving her right knee until it touched Rory's.

His tapping stopped and he shifted his hand until it rested lightly on her thigh. He didn't squeeze, didn't press down, just left it there.

How could such a minimal touch generate so much heat? Somehow she managed to sip her coffee and even contribute to the discussion as warmth from his touch spread, flowing in every direction, affecting her breathing, her heart rate, her sanity.

Kendra finished her pie and glanced at Quinn. "Seconds?"

"No, thanks. But it was delicious, kids." He pushed back his chair. "Don't worry about helping with the dishes tonight. We've got this."

"We absolutely do," Kendra added.

Rory was out of his seat in no time. "If you're sure."

"Very sure. Take off, you two."

Damaris put down her coffee and stood. "Dinner was great. Thank you."

"Aye, thank you." Rory took her hand. "We'll see you in the mornin'."

Damaris glanced at Kendra and Quinn, who were both grinning. What did a person say at a moment like this? She gulped. "'Bye." Then she hurried out the door with Rory.

He started off with ground-eating strides, then caught himself and slowed. "Sorry, lass. I'm a wee bit impatient."

"Do you want to forget about putting on your—"

"Nay, your heart's set on it. I unpacked everythin' before I left the cabin. Made the bed and laid a fire on the hearth, too."

"That was sweet of you."

"I'm partial to makin' love by the warmth of a cracklin' fire. And I'm glad I have a reason to wear everythin' at least once." He smiled. "Dunna expect to have it on long, though."

"At least long enough for me to take a mental picture."

"Ye can take a real one."

"You wouldn't mind?"

"Nay. I'd be honored." After they climbed the steps to the porch, he let go of her hand. "It's best if ye stay here while I put it all on."

"Are you afraid I might tackle you the minute you're naked?"

He smiled. "Maybe I won't be naked. Maybe I'll leave on my briefs."

"Don't you dare. I want the true Scot experience."

"Then that's what ye'll get, lass." He gave her a quick, fierce kiss before going inside.

She moved toward one of the Adirondack chairs but changed her mind. An owl had tuned up in the trees near the cabin. Going back down the steps, she tried to gauge its position. The scent of wood smoke told her Rory had lit the fire before putting on his Scottish duds.

Another owl hooted from a different tree. Maybe they were the same pair she and Rory had heard last night. The soft call went out and was answered. Owl courtship. Was it simple for owls? Or did it seem that way because she didn't know their challenges?

For several minutes the owls were the only sound in the still night. Then another sound was added to the owls' mating call—the chime of a cell phone from inside the cabin. It stopped and Rory's brogue drifted out to her.

Her stomach tightened. Only one person could be calling. His brother. Pulling her cell from her pocket, she checked the time. It was three in the morning in Scotland.

She turned toward the cabin as the door opened and Rory came out, backlit by the light coming through it. Her breath caught. She'd never seen anyone so beautiful in her life.

But he wasn't smiling. Even without his signature grin, though, he was magnificent. His loose cotton shirt was the stuff of romance novel covers. Heck, the entire presentation fit that description.

A length of dark blue and green plaid hung from his shoulder, held there with an ornate pin. The plaid stretched diagonally across his broad chest and disappeared into the waist of the kilt belted around his slim hips.

An embroidered pouch hung from the center of the kilt's belt—the sporran. Kilts had no pockets so the sporran was practical, or so the story went. Why not admit it was a blatant attempt to draw the eye to a man's family jewels? White socks with tassels at the cuff hugged his muscled calves. Soft leather shoes were on his feet.

His chest heaved. "That was Aleck." He came down the steps, his plaid billowing out behind him.

"At three in the morning?"

"Aye." He put his hands on her shoulders and gazed into her eyes. The bleakness in his expression wasn't encouraging.

"What's happened?"

"He just got home. He was in the pub with Catriona's father until the wee hours."

"He was drinking with the opposition?"

"Sometimes that's how matters are settled in Scotland." He took a deep breath. "Catriona's father suggested the meetin' after viewin' a portion of the video Aleck sent him. He's droppin' the charges."

"But that's wonderful! Why do you look so upset?"

"He wants to talk with me, man-to-man, so he can apologize. He knows I won't work for him again, but he wants to introduce me to a friend who owns another distillery. With his recommendation, I'll be guaranteed a good position in the company, one where I could use my brains instead of my muscles. Aleck promised I'd be there to meet with him."

Her stomach pitched. "When?"

"Aleck wants me to strike while the iron's hot. He's already bought my ticket. The plane leaves first thing in the mornin'."

"Rory!"

"I know, lass. But he's fought like a lion for me. I canna refuse to go."

She bit back her protest. "Of course you can't." Lifting her chin, she met his gaze. "But we're damn well going to make the most of tonight."

26

Rory had chafed at the restriction of having only a few days. Now he had mere hours.

"What time do you have to leave the ranch?"

Slipping an arm around her shoulders, he walked with her up the porch steps and over to the door. "Four-thirty. Need to return the rental, go through security." He opened the door and ushered her in.

She took a shaky breath and turned to him. "What about Kendra and Quinn? Should we tell them now?"

"What do you say?" He hated the anguish in her eyes.

"I'm not quite up to it."

"Then we won't."

"Should we get them up in the morning?"

"Nay. I'll text Kendra from the airport."

"Text me from the airport, too. Text me when you have a layover. Then again when you arrive."

His heart broke for her. "I dunna want to think about that, now." He pulled her close. "Not when I'm here, holdin' ye."

She gazed up at him and gradually her expression became resolute. Her glasses made her look even more determined. "You're right. I'm already imagining you gone, but you're not. Not yet."

"Not for hours."

"Seven hours and thirty-six minutes."

"That's bloody exact, isn't it?"

"It's what I do."

"And I love ye for it."

The words registered in her eyes, creating a soft glow that grew brighter.

"You dunna mind me sayin' so?"

She shook her head. Then she reached up and cupped his cheek. "We don't have much time. We should say whatever we want. And do whatever we want."

He tugged her closer. "What d'ye want, lass?"

"To undress you."

"Where's the fun in that?"

"Clearly you've never fantasized about unwrapping a tartan-clad Scotsman."

"That's a fact."

"Well, I have. Will you let me?"

"Aye, if it makes ye happy."

"It will. Stand back and just relax."

"I'll stand back, but I canna promise to relax with your hands roamin' everywhere. Certain parts are tensin' up already."

"Do your best."

"I always aim for that."

"And you succeed very well, Rory McGavin." She crouched in front of him. "Lift your right foot so I can take off your shoe."

Her position recalled their adventure in the barn, but she didn't seem headed in that direction.

She removed his shoes and socks before standing. Grasping the length of material hanging from his shoulder, she held it against her cheek. "So soft."

"Woven from the finest wool. It's called a fly plaid." When they'd set up this modeling session, he'd planned a fitting ending for it. She was moving a wee bit slower than he'd like.

"This looks old." She searched for the fastening on the medallion.

"'Tis old. Passed down from my great-grandparents. Aleck and I each got one."

"It's beautiful." Unfastening it, she carried it over to the small table near the kitchen area. "For safekeeping."

Her concern for a family heirloom touched him. Then again, he'd sensed all along he could trust her with anything that mattered.

She came back, lifted the plaid from his shoulder and tugged it free of his belt. "Where should I put this?"

"On the bed."

Her eyebrows lifted. "You have plans for it?"

"I do."

She pressed her hand to her heart in that endearing way she'd done this morning. When they'd had days instead of hours.

Removing his shirt didn't take her long. She hung it over the same kitchen chair where she'd put his shoes and socks. After she unfastened the sporran, she started to take that over to the table, too.

"Ye might want to keep that handy."

"Handy?

"Leave it by the bed."

Her eyes widened in understanding. "Appropriate." She laid the sporran on the floor near the bed.

"Tucked them in there this afternoon."

"How many?"

"I'm not sayin'."

"It better be a lot." She came back and began unfastening the belt attached to his kilt. "I'm planning to wear you out."

"I'm countin' on it."

"Okay, here we go. The moment of truth, when I discover the answer to that burning question." She pushed the kilt down.

It got hung up on his tadger.

Smiling, she worked the kilt past that jutting impediment and down to his ankles. "You are a true Scot, after all."

"And a randy one." He stepped out of the kilt, picked it up and took it over to the chair with all the rest. "Ye had a turn. Now it's mine."

She looked him up and down as he came toward her. "Do you have a fantasy of undressing an American girl wearing a knit shirt, boots, jeans and plain white underwear?"

"I do, now."

"Doesn't sound exciting to me."

"Ye are not a randy Scotsman." *Who's in love with an American girl wearing a knit shirt, boots, jeans and plain white underwear.*

He gently removed her glasses and left them by the bed with his sporran. She might want them later. She took out her cell phone and he put that there, too, beside his. He'd already set his alarm.

Heat settled in his loins as he cupped her face in both hands and tasted her ripe mouth. He kissed her only long enough to stoke her fire. When she uttered her first moan, he began taking off her clothes, only pausing here and there to nibble on her delicious body so she'd moan some more. How he loved that sound.

When he'd removed everything, he took her hand and led her over to the sturdy bed. "I want to make love to ye while you're lyin' on my plaid."

She lifted her gaze to his. "I was so hoping you would want that."

"Never cared to afore." He spread it out on top of the quilt. Then he scooped her up and laid her in the middle of the soft wool. "Ah, lass, ye look bonnie there. And I want ye so much."

Her throat moved in a slow swallow and her green eyes shimmered with unshed tears. "I want you, too. So very much. That's...that's the problem."

"Only if we make it one." Picking up the sporran, he took out a packet. He held her gaze as he opened it and rolled on the condom. "Some never feel like this, not even for a wee moment."

"I know, but—"

"I'll never regret gettin' to be with ye." Joining her on the bed, he moved between her thighs. "No matter what happens, I'll always be thankful for findin' you, for sharin' somethin' special."

He entered her slowly, tenderly. When he was locked in tight, he balanced on his forearms and leaned down to brush her lips with a gentle kiss. "I love ye, Damaris."

Her voice was choked with tears. "I love you, Rory."

"I'm takin' those words and tuckin' them away in my heart." Easing back, he pushed deep again. "Whenever I'm sad, I'll take them out and remember that a beautiful green-eyed lass said those precious words. It'll be somethin' to hold onto when we're apart.."

"But I want to hold onto *you*." She wrapped him in her arms.

"And so ye are. I'm here and you can hold me all ye want, as tight as ye want." He stroked faster. "Don't think about the mornin'. Be here with me now."

"That's easy to say." Tears leaked from the corners of her eyes. "Not so easy to do."

"'Tis easy. Look at me, lass."

"I'm..." She sniffed. "I'm looking."

"Now feel how I'm lovin' ye." He drove deep.

She sucked in a breath.

"You're safe in this wee cabin, with the cracklin' fire, my soft plaid beneath and me above, bringin' ye pleasure." He willed her to block out everything else.

Then she did. The light in her eyes intensified and her arms tightened around him. The first shudder of her climax rolled over his tadger.

Joy filled his chest nigh to bursting. His rhythm was more purposeful, now. She was with him, arching into each thrust, breathing fast, and...coming...gasping, calling his name over and over.

With one last forceful stroke, he let go. "I love ye, Damaris..." He gulped for air. "*I love ye.*"

Her gaze locked onto his. Her voice was thick with emotion. "I love you, Rory."

He lost track of time as he stayed right where he was. If he moved, if he looked away, would he glance back and find love still shining in her eyes?

But he couldn't hold this position forever. As she'd said...physics. Leaning down, he kissed her gently. "I'll be back."

Her eyes snapped wide. "You will? When?"

His heart ached. "From the lavy."

"Oh." She swallowed. "Silly me."

"Not silly." He brushed his mouth over hers again before he levered himself away and headed for the wee bathroom.

When he returned, she was wrapped in his plaid. It didn't seem like enough, so he reached to the far side of the bed and pulled the quilt over her. Then he climbed in and tugged the other edge of the quilt over his shoulders and backside.

She smiled and nestled against him. "Are you warm enough?"

"Any warmer and I'd be on fire."

"Alrighty, then." She smothered a yawn. "Don't let me go to sleep. I don't want to sleep."

"Neither do I, lass." He combed his fingers through her silky hair. "Where d'ye keep your brush?"

"In my duffel." Her eyelids fluttered closed.

"Maybe I'll fetch it in a bit."

"Okay." She opened her eyes for a moment and then closed them again. "So cozy."

"Mm." Unless he changed the dynamic she'd be asleep soon. She'd asked him not to let that happen, but what kind of man forced a sleepy woman to stay awake so he could make love to her?

Her breathing slowly evened out. He lay very still, memorizing the arch of her brows, the slight tilt at the tip of her nose, the perfection of her cupid's bow mouth, the shape of her chin, the curve of her ear.

No moment ever came again. But some were more precious than others. If only this one could last just a wee bit longer.

27

Damaris woke to an unfamiliar sound—a cell phone tune, but not hers. It ended abruptly and the mattress shifted. *Rory.*

Oh, God, she'd fallen asleep. She sat up. The fire was out but the lamp was still on. "I'm so sorry."

"Dunna be sorry." Leaning over the bed, he cupped her cheek. "Good mornin'." He kissed her lightly.

"How can it be good?"

"I'm still with ye." His long strides took him into the bathroom. A second later water hit the shower walls.

Her stomach hurt. Her chest hurt. Everything hurt. Scrambling out of bed, she tangled herself in his plaid and almost fell. *Slow down.*

Moving carefully, she unwound herself from the soft wool and folded it, making sure the edges were even. She wasn't so careful with her own clothes. She yanked her shirt over her head and shoved her legs into her jeans.

She was dressed by the time he came out of the bathroom with a towel around his hips and his hands full of toiletries. The seductive aroma of his freshly washed body beckoned.

She forced herself to keep her distance. He had a schedule. "What can I do to help?"

"I'll grab some clean clothes." He crossed to his suitcase lying open near the door and tucked his toiletries in a side pocket. "Then if ye could pack the—"

"I will." She carried his plaid over to the table where she'd left the rest of his outfit. After he'd pulled out what he wanted from his suitcase, she carefully tucked in the items she'd taken off the night before.

Thankfully she wasn't crying. She didn't want to get his things wet. Tears might come later, but for now, sorrow weighed on her like a lead x-ray blanket.

She stood. "Done."

"That should do it, then." He tucked his shirt into his jeans, fastened the button at the waist, zipped the fly and buckled his belt. "Wish I could be doin' this in reverse."

She tried to come up with a sassy reply but his imminent departure had taken the sass right out of her. "I was wishing you were getting dressed so we could head to the barn and feed the horses."

"Aye. And look in on wee Eclipse." He held her gaze. "It's all been..."

"Yep." She took a deep breath and glanced away. "We should start down there if you want to pull out of here at four-thirty."

"Right." He crossed to the suitcase.

While he secured the latches, she opened the door and walked into the cool morning. Still dark. The door clicked shut behind her and she started down the steps, her hands shoved in her jeans pockets.

He caught up with her, his suitcase in one hand and his Stetson in the other. "I was hopin' we'd have rain last night." He put on his hat.

"How come?"

"Rain's nice on a metal roof. But I didn't miss it."

"Years ago when I used to sit on the porch and read, sometimes it would rain. I loved that."

"Will ye be stayin' here for the rest of the time or go back to the house?"

Her stomach hollowed out. "I don't know. Why?"

"I'll be thinkin' of ye. Would help to know what to picture."

"Then I'll stay in the cabin."

"Good." He walked to the tiny rental and put his suitcase on the passenger seat. Then he took her hand. "Come 'round to the driver's side with me, lass."

"See if you can stop me." Her voice was scratchy, like she was getting a cold.

He paused by the left side of the car. "See that? I know exactly what side the steerin' wheel's on, now. I'm acclimated."

"You'll be all messed up when you get home."

"That's a fact." He sighed, wrapped her in his arms and cradled her head against his chest. "Nothin' to do with the steerin' wheel issue."

She hugged him so tight her arms ached.

"One more kiss." He lifted her chin, tilted back his hat and lowered his head. When he touched down, he kept the pressure light, his passion restrained.

She responded in kind, letting him know with the gentle movement of her lips that he was cherished. That he was loved.

Slowly he raised his head. His eyes were in shadow, unreadable. He took a breath, as if he might say something. Then he shook his head and released her.

She stepped back so he could open the door. After he did, he touched two fingers to the brim of his hat. Then he took it off, laid it on top of his suitcase and climbed behind the wheel.

As he closed the door, she shoved her hands in her pockets again. He backed out and started down the road without turning on the headlights.

She started after him. Then the headlights flicked on. She stood motionless until she couldn't see them anymore.

"Damaris?"

She turned.

Kendra came down the porch steps and crossed to the parking area. "Where's he going at this hour?"

"He's..." She stopped and cleared her throat. "He's going home."

* * *

Thank God for shoveling horse apples. Damaris would have done all of it, both barns, but she got pushback from Kendra, Zane and Cody. When she ran out of stalls to muck out, she saddled Jake and rode her little heart out. She didn't, however, take the trail to the glen.

Sleeping in the cabin at night, or maybe not sleeping, would be enough of a challenge without adding a ride to the glen. But she'd promised Rory she'd continue to stay there until she left on Saturday.

He'd texted her at his layovers in Chicago and London, then again when he'd landed in Inverness. Since then, nothing. She'd assigned him a special text tone so she wouldn't jump every time her phone chirped.

And it did chirp. A lot. She texted the news to Mandy because that seemed only fair. Mandy agreed to contact everyone who was coming to coffee to let them know it was still on and hugs would be gladly accepted.

Cyber hugs arrived by text on Tuesday and physical hugs on Wednesday afternoon at Pie in the Sky. No one knew what to say, but then, neither did she. The situation sucked and no ready alternatives were available.

Over coffee Mandy announced that Thursday night's plans had changed. Kendra had called a meeting of the Whine and Cheese Club at her house and invited the younger generation. Damaris was fine with whatever. Any distraction was welcome.

Wednesday night it rained, not hard, but enough to make music on the metal roof of the cabin. She broke down and sent Rory a text, even though it was past four in the morning in Inverness. She kept it short. *It's raining. Thinking of you.*

His response was immediate. *Thinking of you, too, lass. Always.*

She hugged the phone to her chest and resisted the urge to send another text. Too much risk of getting maudlin.

Then he sent her a red heart emoji.

She sent one back. And that was it. Enough. More than enough. She fell asleep clutching her phone.

The next morning, she shoveled with a lighter heart. One sweet text exchange and she'd powered up again. After working for a while, she pulled out her phone and looked at their text exchange. No solution had presented itself, and yet... *Always.*

Rory wasn't the type to throw words around that he didn't mean. Hope was still on the table.

She went back to work, grateful for the physical exercise that eased the tension in her muscles and her mind. Then, in mid-shovel, a potential direction for her research appeared, mirage-like at the edge of her consciousness.

She paused, fascinated by the glimmer of an idea. Good Lord, would that work? She examined the concept from every angle as she continued to shovel and rake. Damn, it might be exactly what she'd been looking for, a new way into the subject.

After she finished, she scrounged a spiral-bound notebook from Kendra and sat on the cabin's porch scribbling away. The longer she noodled around, the more promising the idea looked.

She had to tell somebody. Leaving the notebook in the cabin, she scampered down the hill in search of Kendra. She spotted her over by the corral giving a riding lesson. Lessons were normally an hour long.

A quick check of her phone confirmed that the lesson should be almost over. Walking to the house, she grabbed one of the rockers on the porch and waited, rocking impatiently.

Kendra finished the lesson, said goodbye to her student and headed back to the house. "Hey, there! Good to see you sitting for a change, although you're giving the rocker quite a workout."

Damaris stood. "I've been acting pretty crazy, huh?"

"Understandable. Want some coffee?"

"Yes, please. I have something to tell you. Something exciting."

"Excellent! Come on in." Minutes later, she led the way back out to the porch after arming them with coffee and Pie in the Sky brownies. "What's up?"

"I think I've had a breakthrough on my research."

Kendra stared at her. "You're kidding."

"Nope, thought of it while I was mucking out the stalls a while ago. That's why I needed the notebook."

"Hallelujah! I had a hunch and I'm so glad I was right!"

"You did?"

"That used to happen all the time. You'd be working in the barn and come up to the house for scratch paper or a notebook. I got so I expected it. I kept a drawer stocked."

"I did do that, didn't I? I'd forgotten about borrowing the paper. Those ideas always caught me by surprise."

"Do you want to talk about it?"

"Not yet. It's still embryonic, but so much more than I had before. I had to tell you."

"I love seeing you excited about your work again. When you arrived last week, you looked so discouraged. And then..."

"I know. Rory."

"Yeah." Kendra sighed.

"Not much I can do about that. But I think I've just breathed new life into my research project. That helps." She took a deep breath. "It helps a whole lot."

28

Against Rory's objections, Aleck drove him to the airport Thursday morning. "I won't be seein' you for a while, little brother. Least I can do is give you a ride."

"But you'll come and visit, right? I promise you won't have to muck out stalls."

"I'll come. Can't say when, exactly, but I'll make the journey."

"Good."

"Oh, and somethin' else. Ma and Da asked me to talk with you and make sure you want to sell your car."

"I do."

"They'll hold onto it for a while in case you change your mind about this."

"I won't be changin' my mind. Please sell that car. I'm burnin' my boats." It was the code phrase they'd used since childhood for going all in.

Aleck nodded. "Thought so, but I promised I'd check. I'll sell it quick as I can."

"I know it's one more thing for you to handle, but—"

"Not a problem. You'll need some cash while you get your act together."

"Pay yourself first, though. I want to clear my debt."

"Just so you're not sellin' it to pay me."

"I'm not. That's just a bonus."

"I can wait for the money."

"I know you'd do that, and I appreciate it. I'm grateful for everythin' you've done. You worked bloody hard to fix the guddle I got myself into. You keep sayin' it doesn't matter that I turned down that great job, but—"

"It doesn't matter. I'm glad you came back here, though, because I needed to see the change in you and hear the conviction in your voice."

"I didn't have that conviction until the job offer was on the table and I couldn't make myself take it. Before goin' to Montana, I would have snapped it up."

"Then it's a good thing you went to Montana."

"A very good thing."

"I must admit I wish that chemistry degree wasn't down the drain, though."

"It might not be."

"Oh?" Aleck perked up. "There's a distillery near Eagles Nest?"

"Nay. No big operations like that anywhere nearby. But the Guzzlin' Grizzly ought to be brewin' its own beer. I just have to convince them that I'm the man to make that happen."

"You want to make beer instead of single malt?"

He laughed. "It's the Guzzlin' Grizzly, big brother. You don't guzzle single malt. Just means adaptin' my skills, is all."

"I see. That's creative of you. But I'm still not clear. Is it a life in Montana you're after? Or is Damaris mixed in there somewhere?"

"It's the first part I'm goin' for."

"Then why are you rushin' over so you can see her before she leaves?"

"I need to tell her in person about the changes I'm makin'."

"Do you expect her to fall in with your plans?"

"Nay. I'd cut off my right nut before I'd interfere with her work in California."

"But—"

"I've thought it through. If I talk to her in person, I can convince her I'm doin' this for me, for my future. No pressure on her at all. On the other hand, if she chooses to spend more time in Eagles Nest because I'm there…"

"Ah. I can see the wisdom in your plan."

"I can't get any of that across with a phone call."

"So true." Aleck glanced over at him. "I'll miss you like the devil."

"I'll miss you, too. Everyone—Ma, Da, Gran, Grandpa. But—"

"You love her."

"Aye. More than my life."

* * *

The parking lot was full and the house lit up when Rory pulled in a wee bit past eight. What could be happening on a Thursday night? Climbing out of the car, a slightly bigger one this time, he put on his Stetson.

Then he walked toward the path leading up the hill to the cabin. No lights on, no smoke coming from the chimney. So much for his plan to head up there first thing so he could talk with Damaris before seeing anyone else. He'd figured she'd invite him in.

Everything he'd told Aleck was true. An in-person conversation would guarantee she'd understand his motivation for coming back. But he was also looking forward to spending the next two nights with her.

Chances were good she was inside the house partying with whoever was there. Unless she'd decided to leave Eagles Nest already? His gut churned. What if she'd missed him so much she'd taken an earlier flight out?

Hurrying back to the porch steps, he took them two at a time, crossed to the door and banged on the metal knocker.

The door opened and Kendra's laughing face appeared. Her laughter turned to shock. She ducked out the door and closed it quickly behind her. "What are you doing here?"

"I've come back."

"I can see that, but—"

"Is Damaris in there?"

"She is, but listen, Rory, she had a breakthrough on her project today. She's excited about it."

He closed his eyes and sighed. "Thank God. I was afraid missin' me would—"

"She was pretty upset at first. I'd hate to see her get upset again, if you know what I mean."

"I do."

"So I'll ask you again. What the hell are you doing here?"

"I've left Scotland for good."

"Because of Damaris?"

"Nay. Because I want to build a life here."

"What about the dream job your brother found you?"

"Turned it down. This is where I belong. I have plenty to learn, and I'll take whatever jobs I can find until I have the skill to work with horses, either here or somewhere in the area. I—"

"You want to become a cowboy?"

"Aye." He'd save the craft beer idea for another discussion.

"I'll be damned." Her eyes sparkled in the glow from the porch light.

"Aleck is sellin' my car, so eventually I'll have some money to work with. Is there any chance I can rent the cabin? If not, I'll look for somethin' in town."

"You want to rent the cabin?" She said it slowly and the whole time she looked like she was ready to bust out laughing.

"Is that funny?"

"Uh-huh. Or as you might say, it's bloody hilarious. Tell you what, let's go inside."

"Before we do, let me promise you somethin'. I came back now, while Damaris is still here, so I can make sure she understands this isn't about her. I'm not expectin' her to change her life. I would never want that."

She nodded. "Spoken like a true McGavin. Come on in."

"Wouldn't it be better if you asked her to come out here?"

"Oh, no. We all have a stake in this, now. Everybody deserves to hear the new plan." She walked to the door and opened it with a flourish. The first bars of a lively Western tune poured from the sound system. "Hey, listen up!" she called out. "Your favorite Scotsman has returned!"

The room was full of ladies, more than a dozen. They all stopped what they were doing, which looked like some kind of line dance judging from their symmetrical arrangement. The furniture was pushed back and drink glasses were on every surface.

Everyone stared at him, some with their mouths open. Kendra walked over to the source of the music and switched it off. He located Damaris clear across the room.

She looked astonished like everyone else, but happy, too. And so beautiful she made his chest hurt. She'd had a breakthrough on her project. He was overjoyed for her.

Kendra spoke. "As you can see, Rory's back, and I'd like him to tell everyone his new plan."

"You would?" He took off his hat and ran his fingers through his hair.

"Yes, please."

"Well, I..." Tapping his hat against his thigh, he looked around and finally settled his gaze on Damaris. "While I was here I saw a life I wanted more than the life I had in Scotland. I'm a tenderfoot, but I'm determined to become a good hand. And a valuable citizen of Eagles Nest."

Damaris's eyes had turned that luminous green that he loved so much. She clearly approved of his plan, and hers was the most important opinion of all.

He gave her a quick smile before turning to Kendra. "Is that what you meant for me to say?"

"Pretty much. Now tell them where you hope to live."

"You mean about rentin' the cabin?"

"Oh!" Damaris clapped a hand over her mouth.

He glanced at her. "Is that a bad idea?"

The room turned dead silent as she started in his direction. "The cabin is already rented."

"Who's rentin' it?"

"Me."

"*You*?" He scrambled to make sense of it. "Why?"

"I had a breakthrough on my project today."

"I know." The closer she came, the faster his heart pounded.

"As I thought about how it happened, I realized Wild Creek Ranch could be way better for me than a think tank. Kendra's agreed to let me rent the cabin for six months to see if I'm right. We just toasted that decision a little while ago."

He struggled to breathe. "Ye are rentin' the cabin?"

"Yes." She smiled. "But I wouldn't mind having a roommate."

The group erupted with cheers, catcalls and cries of *kiss, kiss, kiss.*

He drew her gently into his arms and tenderly kissed her, afraid any second he'd wake up. But when he lifted his head, she was still there and the group was enthusiastically applauding. "I knew ye could never be lost to me."

"It's this place. It brought us back together."

"Nay, lass. Love brought us back together. This place is special and I'm glad for it." He held her gaze. "But I came back for you."

<u>*Epilogue*</u>

"I just want you to pop over for a wee visit."

Aleck gazed across the desk at his mother, who'd made a trip to town specifically to make this request. "I'd planned to go sometime, Ma. But he's only been there a couple of weeks. I think I should wait, let him get his feet under him before I show up."

She sighed. "You're right. It's only that he seems very serious about her. I'm sure she's lovely, but it feels so strange for him to be livin' with someone I've never laid eyes on."

"It's strange for me, too. But everything he says makes me believe that she's right for him."

"I agree. But if you went over there, you'd know that for yourself. And you could tell me. I'm dyin' to go over, but that could send the wrong message, like I'm checkin' out my prospective daughter-in-law."

He laughed. "Which is exactly what you'd be doin'."

"Of course, which is why I can't go. But you can get away with it much easier. So how long do you think it'll be before he gets his feet under him?"

"That's hard to say."

"I estimate about two months."

"Oh, you do, do you?"

"Yes. Two months is plenty of time for him to get settled. What's your schedule like?"

"I'll have to look." He got why she was agitating for this. Rory was a grown man but he was still her baby boy. He'd never been this far away for this long. And he'd never been head-over-heels in love. "I'll see what I can do, Ma."

"I just need—"

"Don't worry. I'll come back with a full report."

She smiled. "Thank you, son."

Tansy gave Aleck a smile and slid behind the wheel. "I can't help help noticing that you have a lot of questions about this way of life."

He flashed her a grin. "Askin' questions is second nature to me. It's how I make my livin'."

"Yes, but—"

"It's also my knee-jerk response to somethin' that's completely foreign to me. When I'm out of my depth, I Hoover up everythin' I can."

"Fair enough."

"I'm happy so many are goin' tonight. Gives me a chance to buy a round. I'm very good at orderin' beer."

"Good luck with that. You might have to arm-wrestle a couple of McGavins first."

"That could be interestin'. I used to do quite a bit of that. Haven't lately. I think I could take Cody, possibly Trevor, but if they put me up against Ryker, chances are I'm goin' down."

"It's his military bearing."

"Nay, it's his muscles. He's built for the caber toss."

"I don't know what that is, but if it involves brute strength, Ryker's up to it."

"The caber toss is one of the main events in the Highland games."

"And a caber is..."

"A log the size of a telephone pole."

"Wow. Have you ever done it?"

"Oh, yeah. Rory and I had to prove ourselves to be manly men." He chuckled. "Can't say we did it well, but we did it. Caber toss, hammer throw, shot put. We gave them all a go."

"Wearing kilts?"

"Aye. That's how it's done."

"Any videos?" Surely someone had recorded that for posterity.

"God, I hope not."

Damn. "Listen, if you've managed to toss a telephone pole without injuring yourself, you shouldn't take a back seat to any of these cowboys."

"Aye, but I've never ridden a horse, now, have I?"

"You'd be fine."

"That's what Rory says."

"It's no different from the caber toss and that other stuff you mentioned. You do it so you can say you did."

"Are you throwin' down a gauntlet, lass?" He sounded amused.

"I might be. I'm on the evening shift for the next few days so my days are free. How about going for a ride with me?"

"Well..."

"I dare you."

He started laughing.

"I double-dog dare you."

Now he was laughing so hard he could barely talk. "Never heard that one." He gulped for air. "Sounds...very...serious."

"Oh, it is. You don't back down from a double-dog dare unless you want to lose your manly man standing."

Clearing his throat, he glanced over at her. "You win. I'll go ridin'."

New York Times bestselling author Vicki Lewis Thompson's love affair with cowboys started with the Lone Ranger, continued through Maverick, and took a turn south of the border with Zorro. She views cowboys as the Western version of knights in shining armor, rugged men who value honor, honesty and hard work. Fortunately for her, she lives in the Arizona desert, where broad-shouldered, lean-hipped cowboys abound. Blessed with such an abundance of inspiration, she only hopes that she can do them justice.

For more information about this prolific author, visit her website and sign up for her newsletter. She loves connecting with readers.

VickiLewisThompson.com